Norah McClintock

MISTAKEN IDENTITY

**Other Scholastic books by
Norah McClintock:**

Shakespeare and Legs

The Stepfather Game

Jack's Back

Norah McClintock

Mistaken Identity

Cover by
Laura Fernandez

Scholastic Canada Ltd.

Scholastic Canada Ltd.
123 Newkirk Road, Richmond Hill, Ontario, Canada L4C 3G5

Scholastic Inc.
555 Broadway, New York, NY 10012, USA

Ashton Scholastic Limited
Private Bag 94407, Greenmount, Auckland, New Zealand

Scholastic Australia Pty Limited
PO Box 579, Gosford, NSW 2250, Australia

Scholastic Ltd.
Villiers House, Clarendon Avenue, Leamington Spa
Warwickshire CV32 5PR, UK

Canadian Cataloguing in Publication Data

McClintock, Norah
    Mistaken identity

ISBN 0-590-24627-5

I. Title.

PS8575.C55M537 1995   jC813'.54   C95-930985-3
PZ7.M33Mi 1995

7 6 5 4 3 2 1   Printed in Canada   5 6 7 8/9

And after all, what is a lie?
'Tis but the truth in masquerade.

—Lord Byron

Chapter One

Mitch Dugan crumpled the morning newspaper into a hard little ball and shoved it into the kitchen garbage. As he reached for the eggs, he said, "Are you crazy? Do you know what kind of trouble a thing like that can cause?" He cracked an egg so forcefully on the edge of the cast-iron skillet that the shell shattered into dozens of pieces, which fell onto the counter and into the skillet. "Damn," he muttered. He grabbed a rag from under the sink to clean up the mess.

Zanny watched him with dismay. What was he so mad about? "It's not like I did anything illegal," she said. "It was just a *little* protest."

"A *little* protest?" Her father cracked another egg into the skillet, more cautiously this time. "Do you know who you sound like when you say that? You sound exactly like your friend Lily."

Zanny flinched at the mention of the name. A

wave of sadness washed over her.

"I would have expected a stunt like this from Lily. I expected a lot more common sense from you."

"But I didn't *do* anything," Zanny protested. "I was just standing up for something I believe in. Don't you care about that? I was making a point. If people just continue doing what they're doing, polluting — "

Her father shook his head impatiently. "You're not listening to me, Zanny. You're not hearing what I'm telling you. I have no problem with you standing up for what you believe in. I have no problem with you defending the environment. But I have a very big problem with stunts like this. If you want to make a point, find a better way to do it. Don't go around organizing demonstrations, blocking traffic, getting your picture in the paper. . . . "

"But it was a peaceful demonstration. And it was completely legal. The police were there, and they didn't arrest anyone. All they did was direct traffic. I didn't do anything wrong." She felt like she was pressing the replay button. She'd been telling him the same thing over and over again all morning.

Zanny's father looked sharply at her. She was sure he was going to shout some more. But he didn't. Instead, he shook his head, sighed and said, "I don't want you getting involved in any more protests, okay? And no more pictures in the paper." He turned off the gas under the pan of scrambled eggs. "Are you sure you don't want any?"

Zanny wrinkled her nose. Her father had always favoured hearty breakfasts. She used to share them with him when she was little. But lately, the smell of food so early in the morning made her stomach churn. The most she could handle was a mug of sugared tea and a slice of toast.

Her father dropped down onto a chair and reached for the ketchup bottle. Zanny stared into her tea. Ketchup on eggs. All her life her father had been putting ketchup on eggs, and all her life it had made her want to look away. It made her think of flesh and blood.

"I want you to give me your word," her father said. "I want you to promise me, no more demonstrations."

Zanny looked down into the black surface of her tea and into the blackness of her eyes in its reflection. She had thought he'd changed. She had thought she'd grown up enough for him to have left all that nonsense behind. But he was making her promise again, as he'd always done. When he said, "No more demonstrations," she heard all the other promises he had begged her to make over the years: no more taking off after school with her friends without telling him exactly where she was, who she was with and when she would be home; no more hanging around with kids her father hadn't met — met, and grilled, like steaks on a barbecue; no talking to strangers, defined not as people she didn't know, but as people *he* didn't know. He drove her so crazy about that one sometimes she could just scream. In fact, she *had* screamed, more than once: "I know hundreds of people you don't know. My life is filled with them. What are you going to do when I go away to school? Quiz the whole student body?"

"Zanny?" he said now. "Promise me. This is important."

"But why? What did I do that was so terrible?"

"You want to go to college, don't you?"

Zanny nodded. In fact, she couldn't wait to go. She had only one more year of high school left.

"Well, then," he replied, "you don't want anything on your record that makes you look like a troublemaker. The competition to get into a good school is pretty tough these days. The competition for scholarships is even tougher. . . . "

"But, Dad . . . "

"No more demonstrations, okay?"

Zanny sighed. She could argue with him, but he would just argue right back. And he would continue until he wore her down — he always did. He would keep on at her until she either agreed with him or was forced to lie to him. She didn't like to do it, but sometimes he left her no choice. She thought back to a unit on ethics she'd done in civics class a few months ago. A lot of kids had been bored by it, but not Zanny. She'd found it fascinating, especially when Mr. Mercer had explained something called mental reservation. What a great idea that was. You could say to someone, "No, I don't think you're a jerk," and as long as you added to yourself, without even speaking the words aloud, *At least, not all the time,* no one could accuse you of lying. Because, according to the principle of mental reservation, if you didn't lie to yourself, you weren't lying at all.

"Zanny, did you hear me? I want you to promise me you won't get involved in any more protests."

"Okay, I promise," Zanny said. "No more

protests." *At least*, she added to herself, *not today*.

Her father nodded and forked some ketchup-drenched eggs into his mouth. "Good girl." He reached over and squeezed her hand, and suddenly she felt guilty about lying. She felt angry, too, that he'd forced her into it. Why couldn't he just let her do what she wanted to do? Why did he have to be so overprotective?

She gulped down the rest of her tea and stood up abruptly. "I have to go," she said.

He looked surprised. "So early?"

"I promised to meet Sheri, to help her with her chemistry homework."

Zanny threw on her jacket, grabbed her book bag and let herself out of the house before her father could say anything else. She didn't relax until she was halfway down the long gravel driveway. Then she drew in a deep breath, gazed around and felt the knot in her stomach slowly begin to dissolve. Whenever her father drove her crazy with his worrying, all she had to do was step outside and take a good long look at the view. It always calmed her.

May 15

Chuck Benson washed down the last of a sugar-glazed doughnut with a gulp of coffee, double-cream, double-sugar, from Donut King. He wiped the chips of sugar glaze from his lips as he reached for a stack of newspapers from the northeastern part of the country. They weren't big-city dailies — you had to have seniority with the agency to get those — they were weeklies or twice-a-weeklies from small places you never heard of unless you happened to live there or had a relative who did. Chuck didn't have much seniority — yet. And what seniority he planned to get in the years to come, he didn't intend to accumulate tucked away in the basement of the newspapers and periodicals subsection of the information-gathering division of the intelligence department of the agency.

Chuck Benson worked through his stack of small-town papers with machine-like precision. He knew what to read — any news items with names in them — and what to skip — politics, lifestyles columns (except for social columns), opinion pieces, editorials. He knew what to look at — photographs, mainly — and what to ignore — ads, cartoons, crossword puzzles. He could make his way through a newspaper in one-third less time than anyone else in the department. But then, Chuck was more ambitious than anyone else. Chuck Benson would show them what he was made of. At least, that was the plan.

He had come into the newspapers and periodicals subsection thinking that after a month, they'd promote him for sure. Fifteen months later, he was still plowing his way through a metre-high stack of small-town newspapers every day. Lately there had been days when, munching his mid-morning doughnut and gulping his double-double from Donut King, he asked himself, who am I kidding? The way things are going, I'll never get out of here. The spiders will start to spin webs from me, my hair will turn white, I'll be sitting here until I retire.

He scanned page one of a weekly from upstate

New York, then turned to page two and quickly ran his finger down the columns of type, ignoring everything that wasn't a name. His finger stopped at a two-column photograph of a bunch of kids holding picket signs. He shook his head. No matter how great things were in America, there were always kids protesting something, somewhere. This time it was the use of styrofoam packaging by a local burger joint. Save Our Environment, the signs read. Save the Planet Earth. Say No to Instant Garbage.

Then one of the faces in the photograph caught Chuck's eye. He looked at it, then dismissed it. It couldn't be. What were the chances he could open up some hick-town newspaper and find himself staring at his winning ticket, his pass to success? The odds against it had to be a million to one.

He looked at the photograph again and studied the girl's face closely. She was young, maybe fifteen or sixteen, which, he realized, was about the right age. Her hair looked light in the black-and-white photograph; she looked like a blonde, not a brunette. But apart from the hair, which was really nothing to go on these days, everything else set off alarms. The large wide eyes, the pert nose, the generous mouth, turned down in disapproval in this photograph, those cheekbones. Except for one other place, he had never seen cheekbones like those before.

Chuck swung his chair around to the computer terminal and keyed in his identification number and password. Using a mouse to slip through the files on the computer screen, he located the MPCGAU file and entered his authorization code, a second identification number, and two more passwords.

Looking at the pictures on the screen was strange. The first time Chuck had seen the file, he had looked sceptically at Ed Nolan, who had gone through training with him. "They can't be serious," he had said. "How can a computer take a picture of a ten-year-old and transform it into the same person, twenty-five years later?" That was what the Missing Persons Computer-Graphics-Assisted Update file did. "How do they know it even works? How do they know that what the computer does is accurate?"

"I took the tour," Nolan answered. "It keys in on bone structure, and mixes in genetics and the laws of probability. Trust me, it works."

But Chuck hadn't believed it. Not until two days later when Ed Nolan gave him a photograph. "This is me as a kid," he said. "My dad took it when I was eight years old." Then he handed Chuck a piece of plain bond paper with a computer image lasered onto it. "This is the picture the computer kicked out after we fed it the photo of me as a kid."

Chuck stared at the startling likeness of Ed the computer had generated. Since that day, he'd been a believer. But it was still weird to think that a computer could take a picture of a child and accurately transform it into an adult of almost any age. It was like predicting the future.

He flipped through the file, ignoring the small images in the upper right-hand corner of the screens. This was where digitized versions of original photographs of children were housed, the "befores." He concentrated instead on the "afters" — the computer-generated versions of what those people

10

would look like now, if they were still alive. He flipped through dozens of "befores" and "afters" until he found the one he was looking for. Then he picked up the newspaper again and looked at the girl in the demonstration photo. He stared at it, then at the "after" image filling most of the computer screen. Well, if it wasn't her, it was her twin sister; that was the only way two people could look so much alike. Which meant there was a very good chance that he had just earned himself a promotion — because, when nobody else had been able to, he had found Mike Alexander's kid. And where Mike Alexander's kid was, Mike Alexander probably was, too.

* * *

Special Agent Hank Wiley leaned back in his chair and swivelled his head from side to side to relieve the tension that had been building in his neck for the past hour. He hated paperwork. He'd always hated it. Only now it wasn't paperwork any more. He hardly saw a piece of paper from one day to the next. Now everything was done on computers. But it amounted to the same thing. A form was a form, whether it was printed on paper or displayed on a screen. Forms existed to be filled out. And the boys in the big offices upstairs were real sticklers for forms. Wiley made a sour face. This wasn't why he had joined the agency. He'd been looking for a little excitement, not a wagonload of forms to fill out.

He stretched out one powerful arm and glanced at the watch strapped to his wrist. Almost five o'clock.

The phone at his elbow jangled. Shoot, Wiley

thought. A couple of minutes more and I could have been out of here. Who would call at five-fifty-five — no, make that five-fifty-eight — on a Friday afternoon? He grabbed the receiver.

"Wiley here."

"Special Agent Wiley? This is Benson. Chuck Benson. Down in N and P."

"N and *what?*" Wiley didn't know what the guy was talking about, and at a few minutes to quitting time on Friday, he didn't care. "Look, Benton," he began.

"Ben*son*," the voice on the other end of the line said.

"Whatever. Look, pal, I'm just on my way out the door. How about I give you a jingle Monday morning? Whatever it is, I'm sure it can keep until then, right?"

"Well, I guess," Benson said. He sounded deflated. "But the flag on the file said Immediate Contact, so naturally . . . "

Wiley's interest flared. Immediate Contact. Only hot files rated that flag. Whatever Benson had, it wasn't routine. It might even be something interesting.

"Where did you say you were calling from, Benson?"

"N and P. Newspapers and Periodicals. In Intelligence. It's about an MPCGAU file."

"An MP file?" Wiley leaned over to his computer. "What file are we talking about, Benson?" Benson rattled off the file number and Wiley entered it. He looked at the small digitized photo in the upper corner. Then his eyes skipped down to the bottom of the screen. He read the name: Melissa Alexander. Then the "missing since" date. He shook his head. It was true what they said — the days were long, but the years flew by. Had it really been thirteen years? He stared at the larger image on the screen, the one that showed Melissa Alexander as she would look now.

"What about her, Benson?" he said into the phone. "Don't tell me you actually located the kid?"

There was a slight pause on the other end of the line. Then, in a voice no longer deflated, Chuck Benson replied, "As a matter of fact, I did."

Suddenly, Hank Wiley forgot all about the paperwork and his weekend plans. He forgot he was tired. Suddenly Hank Wiley felt full of energy, like he was the luckiest man in the world, with the best job in the world — and all because some underpaid mole down in the bowels of Intelligence had stumbled on the whereabouts of Mike Alexander's kid.

* * *

Everett Lloyd towelled his rusty red hair, slapped some aftershave onto his cheeks, opened the bathroom door and almost had a heart attack. His daughter Trish, his son Rob and his wife Margaret all rushed toward him, yelling, "Surprise!"

"Happy birthday, Dad!" Rob said, thrusting a box at Everett. Trish jumped up and down.

"Open it now, Daddy," she begged. "You'll never guess what it is! Open it now!"

In fact, Everett Lloyd guessed exactly what was in the box the instant Rob handed it to him. He could tell from the size of the box, from its shape and its weight. It was another car for his antique train set. Margaret had been buying him a piece every year since they were married — ten years ago now. For most of the six years of her life, Trish had been more excited than Everett by the gifts. Everett had always been careful not to puncture that excitement.

"Well," he said, hefting the brightly wrapped package for Trish's benefit, "I wonder what it could be." He held up the smallish box and shook it.

"Be careful, Daddy," Trish shrieked. "You'll break it."

Everett arched an eyebrow. "Oh? It's something breakable?"

"Come on, Dad," Rob said. "You know what it is." Rob was nine now, a man of the world.

"He does not!" Trish cried. "And don't you dare tell him."

Everett gave the box a more solid shake. Then he set the package down on the small hall table and unwrapped it. Trish glowed with anticipation.

"It's so beautiful, Daddy. You're really going to love it. I know you are."

Everett lifted the lid from the box and pulled out the wadded newspaper protecting the contents. He caught his breath when he removed the last twist of newsprint. This year he really *was* surprised. This year Margaret had outdone herself.

He lifted the sleek black locomotive from its box in utter amazement. He had seen ones like this only in magazines. Over a hundred years old, they were as rare as they were expensive.

"Wherever did you find it?" he asked as he turned the locomotive over and over in his hand.

"*I* didn't find it," Margaret said. "Louise did." Louise Rafferty, Margaret's closest friend, was an antiques dealer. "She spotted it in a little shop in upstate New York on a buying trip last month. She told me about it and arranged for it to be sent down here. I was afraid it wouldn't arrive in time for your birthday."

Everett caught her in his arms, kissed her and spun her around. Then he kissed Trish, who squealed with delight. To Rob he said, "How about helping me clean up this mess? I have to get to work." Rob nodded. Together they scooped up the discarded wads of newspaper and stuffed them into a wastepaper basket. Then something caught Everett's eyes. A face. A face in a photograph of a group of protesters. He flattened out the newspaper, smoothed the creases and peered at the picture again.

"Dad?"

"Huh?" He could hardly tear himself away from that face. The eyes haunted him. And those cheekbones. He had only seen one other person with cheekbones like that.

"Hey, are you okay, Dad?" Rob asked. "You look like you've seen a ghost."

Everett forced a laugh and ruffled his son's hair. "I'm fine, just fine. But I'm running late, Rob. I have to get to the office. Do me a favour, finish cleaning this up, will you?"

Rob nodded.

When Everett Lloyd left the house, he had the newspaper photo carefully folded in his pocket.

* * *

Before moving to Birks Falls, Zanny and her father had lived in at least a dozen places that Zanny could remember, maybe more that she couldn't. Mostly they had been in big cities — Newark, Detroit, Cincinatti, Phoenix, Dallas. But the place she liked best of all was Birks Falls.

What she liked most was its smallness. It had only two major employers — a vegetable cannery and a district health centre. Her father worked as an orderly at the latter.

She also liked the country environment — walking down the sloping driveway on an early spring morning like this one, the grass around her, the gravel underfoot, ankles all lost in the morning mist. She could look down and around, across a sweeping expanse of long grass, and see the twinkle of the light in Mrs. Finster's kitchen a couple of hundred metres away in one direction and the twinkle of the light in Mr. Taylor's bedroom a few hundred yards the opposite way. If she looked hard enough and the mist was thin enough, she could see the cluster of lights in town, way down the road. There was none of the bustle of rush-hour traffic that used to assault her before she even got out of bed in Newark, none of the acrid smog that filled her lungs in Detroit. As she strolled down the driveway in Birks Falls, she heard the melody of the jays and robins and inhaled the tang of the damp long grass and the sweetness of clover. Of all the places she had ever lived, none was as beautiful as this.

When they had first moved here and Zanny had seen the place, she had prayed that her father would never move them again. For once, her prayers were answered. Her father seemed to like Birks Falls. The fact that they had stayed here for more than a year was proof. And although he was still overprotective, even that was easing. It seemed to Zanny that her father was slowly relaxing. Even last week's upset about the picture in the paper was nothing compared to some of the explosions they had been through together. There was no doubt in her mind: the peace and quiet of this place was having a positive effect on both of them. Her father had found a job he liked. Although how anyone could actually *like* being an orderly — bathing sick people, carrying bedpans, pushing wheelchairs — she didn't know.

Zanny had even made friends in Birks Falls. Well, one friend. Her first ever *best* friend. The promise of the morning faded as she thought of Lily. It all seemed so ironic. For as long as Zanny could remember, she had been moving around with her father; she had always been the new kid in class; she had always been the one making that long walk down the aisle in yet another classroom among yet another bunch of strange faces to yet another assigned seat. Then, about a week after Zanny had started school in Birks Falls, Lily had arrived. She strode into class that first day as if she'd been entering strange classrooms all her life. If she felt nervous, it didn't show on her round, open face. Lily met each and every pair of eyes that lit on her with a large, confident grin. Zanny had been so impressed by her self-assurance that she found herself smiling right back, which seemed to be all the encouragement Lily needed. As soon as homeroom ended, Lily came up to Zanny and suggested that they have lunch together. They ate together every day until one day it sank in. I have a friend, Zanny realized. For the first time in my life, I have someone I can confide in, someone who confides in me. That same day, Zanny started to pray that her father wouldn't come home and announce that he had quit his job, that he wouldn't start packing their suitcases again.

It had never occurred to her that Lily's father might be the one to do the packing, that Lily might be the one to move away. And so far away — not to another town or another state, but to another country. Lily's father, an engineer, had taken a two-year position in Germany. Before Lily had left, she and Zanny had decided what colleges they would both apply to. They had promised each other they would be roommates. They exchanged letters at least twice a month. But it just wasn't the same. As she strolled down the road toward town and school, Zanny wondered what her chances were of finding another friend like Lily.

Chapter Two

May 20

Zanny caught a glimpse of the boy from the corner of her eye. Her heart hammered in her chest; her pulse raced. The long hallway was deserted, except for the two of them. And he was standing right next to the exit. To leave the building, she would have to pass him. Her knees weakened at the prospect. She would never be able to do it. She would probably die. Her heart would seize up and she would drop like a stone to the cold, hard floor.

She reached for her book bag and slung it over her shoulder. Then, forcing a calm she didn't feel, she closed her locker door and secured it. She adjusted the strap of her book bag, drew in a deep breath, held her head high and turned around.

He was gone.

She couldn't believe it. He'd been there, and now he had vanished. Slowly her pulse returned to normal; her shoulders slumped as she trudged down the hallway. It was her own fault, she thought. Opportunity had knocked, but instead of opening the door and inviting it in, she had stupidly pretended not to hear. What was it that Mr. Atkinson always said? "He who hesitates, ladies and gentlemen, is lost." Or, in this case, *has* lost.

Zanny sighed and stepped out into the warm afternoon. She had actually been presented with a chance to go right up to the new guy, unobserved, and to talk to him, something she'd imagined herself doing every day and night for the past three days, ever since he had walked into her algebra class. But instead of seizing the opportunity, she had flinched. He who hesitates, ladies and gentlemen, is lost.

She rounded the side of the school, angry with herself, and almost collided with someone. It was him.

"I . . . I . . . " she stammered. Her face turned red. "I'm sorry."

He smiled. His eyes were the deepest, richest brown she'd ever seen, like chocolate. His hair was an almost perfect match. It was thick and glossy and swept back from his broad forehead. His mouth was wide and generous. His teeth flashed white.

"No, really," he said, "*I'm* sorry. I didn't mean to startle you."

"It . . . it's okay." Zanny felt so embarrassed. She had never stammered before, not even standing in front of a crowd of people to give the manager of the Burger Shack a piece of her mind. And now here she was, stammering like a pathetic child, tongue-tied. "It . . . it was an accident."

His face suddenly took on a sheepish look. "I

don't know if I'd exactly call it an accident," he volunteered. "The truth is, I was kind of waiting in ambush for you."

Her pulse quickened. "You were?"

He nodded. "The fact is, I've been watching you for the past couple of days."

Zanny couldn't believe her ears. The guy Sheri had been drooling over all week had instead been looking at her, Zanny Dugan.

"I'm new around here," he said.

She knew. Every girl in the entire school knew.

"I'm Nick. Nick — "

"Mulaney," she said. "I know." He looked so surprised that she blushed. "I'm Zanny —"

"Dugan," he finished, and smiled. "Zanny's a nice name. Unusual. Is it short for something?"

"Alexandra."

"Nice." He smiled again, and she found herself unable to look away from his chocolate eyes. "Look, Zanny, I hope you don't think I'm being too pushy. I mean, you hardly know me. You don't know anything about me except my name and the fact that I sit behind you in algebra. But I was wondering — do you think maybe we could have lunch together or something?"

She stared at him, stunned.

"We could meet in the cafeteria," he added quickly. "That way, if you decide you can't stand me, you won't be stuck with me. What do you say? I'd really like to get to know you." He grinned. "Not to mention I could use a little help with my algebra."

Every word Nick spoke echoed, as if it were coming from a long distance. Zanny still couldn't believe this was happening. He had more than three hundred girls to choose from — well, maybe half that number if you subtracted the sophomores and the frosh — yet, for some reason, she was the one he wanted to have lunch with.

"You don't have to give me an answer right now," he continued. "Tell you what — I'll be down in the cafeteria at first period lunch tomorrow . . . " His eyes clouded. "You do have first period lunch, don't you?"

Zanny nodded.

"Okay. I'll be there. Think it over. If you want to, you can join me. If not, well . . . " He shrugged. "Let's just say I hope you decide to join me." Before she could even catch her breath to attempt an answer, Nick was looking at his watch. "Hey, I gotta run. My old man's going to have a fit if I don't get the garage cleaned out by supper time." He grinned. "A nice guy, my old man. But very strict."

Zanny smiled wryly. "He sounds a lot like my dad."

"Well, see you. I hope."

"Yeah," Zanny said under her breath as she watched him stride away. "I hope."

* * *

For the first few blocks, Zanny walked on air. She had noticed Nick Mulaney from his first day at school. They all had, she and Sheri and Michelle and Anna. The Swim Girls. Sheri, Michelle and Anna were the closest thing Zanny had to friends now that Lily was gone, but the truth was, they weren't that close. She didn't click with them the way she had with Lily. She couldn't confide in them as she had confided in Lily, and she knew they shared confidences with each other that they didn't share with her. It didn't surprise her. The three of them had much more in common with each other than they did with her. They had all lived in Birks Falls their whole lives. Their parents all knew each other. And they were all on Birks Falls' famous synchronized swim team. They spent ten hours a week in the pool together, preparing for local competitions and state championships. Still, they invited Zanny to eat lunch with them, and even if they weren't connected to her the way Lily had been, they kidded around with her and talked about boys with her. Lately they'd been talking about Nick Mulaney.

"He's beautiful," Sheri had enthused that first day, chewing the nail on her little finger while she stared at him.

"He probably has a girlfriend," Michelle said with a sigh.

"He just moved here," Sheri countered. "I heard from Darlene . . ."

"You *heard?*" Zanny said.

Sheri shrugged. "Okay, so I asked." Darlene was one of the administrative assistants in the school office. "She said he just moved here from Chicago. Even if he does have a girlfriend, she's half a country away. And we, ladies, are here. Which means that we have what they call the hometown advantage. So stand back, one and all, and watch Sheri do her stuff. I'm gonna rope this one, and I'm gonna ride him all the way to the prom."

Anna arched a feathery chestnut eyebrow. "Maybe," she shot back. "Or maybe someone else will lasso him right out from under you."

Michelle groaned. "Here we go again. The famous Chastell–Arthurs rivalry. He looks like a nice guy, and I feel sorry for him. He doesn't know what he's just landed in the middle of."

Zanny had laughed. She'd also wondered why the guys always fell for it. They were always so dazzled they couldn't look at any other girls.

Sheri and Anna had really gone at it this time. Exactly twenty-four hours after first laying eyes on their prey, they were both stalking him. And now Zanny was amused and not a little pleased to find out that this time the prey hadn't succumbed to either of the great hunters. The two of them would absolutely choke when they heard that Zanny was having lunch with Nick Mulaney tomorrow. Hey, and who knows, maybe *she* would be the one to ride him all the way to the prom.

Then Zanny faltered. Suddenly she wasn't walking on air any more. Suddenly she was right back on hard, boring terra firma. Sure, she could go to the prom with Nick — *if* he asked her, and *if* her father gave his permission, which was the bigger of the two *if*s. All her father would require was for Nick to have moved to town three *months* ago, not three days ago, and for him to have submitted himself for inspection every single day since. Her father would then, of course, have asked him a couple of million questions. The inquisition he submitted her friends to was almost creepy. "I'm just playing it smart," he said when she complained. "These days you can't be too careful."

Well, there was no point in worrying about it now. Look on the bright side, Zanny told herself, maybe Nick will decide you're not his type, maybe the whole issue of the spring prom will never come up. But if it did, well, this time she was determined to win. She wasn't a child any more. She was sixteen. And she was every bit as good a judge of character as her father. She could make her own decisions. That's what she would tell him. "In a year I'm going to college, Dad, I'm going to *have* to make my own decisions. How can I ever learn to do that when you won't let me practise? Besides, Dad, we're talking about a high school prom. What's the worst thing that could happen?" That Nick will dump me, probably. Or that he'll never ask me in the first place.

* * *

Zanny saw the flashing lights from the bottom of the hill. An ambulance, two police squad cars and one other car, which looked ordinary except for the red lights flashing on its roof, appeared to be clustered at the bottom of her driveway. But that didn't make sense. Surely they were there for one of the neighbours — old Mr. Taylor, all alone except for a half-dozen cats and a son-in-law who visited every second Sunday, or Mrs. Finster, a widow with three grown children: a dentist, a professor and a rabbi. Maybe Mr. Taylor had had a heart attack. Maybe Mrs. Finster had fallen down the stairs. Zanny quickened her pace, telling herself that nothing could possibly have happened at her house that would bring out an ambulance and two police cars, but wanting to be sure anyway.

Then, when she was close enough, she suddenly stopped. All those cars were definitely in front of *her* house. Something had happened there. Something bad. Zanny started to run.

A length of yellow crime-scene tape stretched across the front porch and ran around to the side and back of the house. On the east side of the house, two police officers were studying the ground beneath the kitchen window.

Zanny had one leg over the tape when a voice boomed at her, "Hey, you, kid, where do you think you're going?" Zanny hesitated, but only for a moment. This was *her* house. She swung her other leg over the yellow tape and started up the steps to the front door.

"Hey!" the voice shouted behind her. "Stop or I'll arrest you for impeding a police investigation."

Zanny ground to a halt, but not because the voice had threatened her. She stopped because she had found herself nose-to-chest with a burly plainclothes policeman.

"Whoa, there, young lady," he said. "Where do you think you're going?"

"I live here," Zanny answered. "This is my house." Then a thought occurred to her. "Where's my father? Have you called my father? Is he home from work yet?"

"What's your name?" the big policeman asked. His voice was gentle now; it had lost all trace of irritation.

Zanny told him.

"I'm Lieutenant Jenkins," he said. "Are you just getting home from school?"

Zanny nodded. "What happened? Did someone break in?"

"That's what we're trying to find out." Lieutenant Jenkins stepped aside to let her enter.

The small house was overflowing with people. One police officer was speaking on the telephone just inside the kitchen door. Two more were huddled in the foyer, talking in low voices. A flash went off. Zanny peered into the living room and saw a photographer with a police officer's badge hanging from his belt, taking pictures.

"Hey, Jenkins!" called the man on the phone. "The captain wants to talk to you."

Lieutenant Jenkins nodded. "Listen, Zanny," he said, "I want you to do me a favour, okay?"

Zanny nodded. Why was he looking at her like that? Why was he staring through her like that?

"I want you to stand here," Lieutenant Jenkins continued. "Just stand here and don't move until I come back. I won't be long. You think you can do that for me, Zanny?"

The urgency in his voice unsettled her, the kindergarten-simple wording of his request irked her, but she nodded.

"Good," he said. "Good girl." As he turned his attention to the phone, Zanny surveyed the troop of men in the house, forming and reforming into knots in the foyer, in the living room, in the kitchen. She glanced at the clock on the hall table. Nearly five, it read. She wondered again where her father was, and whether the police had called him.

The police photographer came out of the living room, tucking a roll of film into a camera bag.

Another man, this one dressed in white, pushed himself away from the wall he had been leaning against.

"You guys through in there?" he asked the photographer. "Can we bag it now?"

White shirt. White pants. White shoes. He belonged to the ambulance. An ambulance meant that someone had been hurt. The burglar, perhaps? But how? Had he been surprised by the police? Mrs. Finster was the eyes and ears of the neighbourhood. She knew everything that went on and never hesitated to intervene when she thought it necessary, which was usually. Maybe Mrs. Finster had seen someone break into the house, and had called the police, and they had come and caught the burglar in the act. Maybe there had been a shootout and he had been wounded. Maybe a police officer had been hurt.

Zanny took a few steps toward the living room, consumed now by curiosity, wondering who had been hurt and how badly.

She felt as though she had stepped onto the set of a television detective show. A man was lying face down on the floor outlined with white tape, which meant that he wasn't just injured, he was dead. Zanny's knees buckled. A dead man was lying on her living room floor, and blood from his wound had seeped onto the sand-coloured carpet. Then the ambulance attendant turned the body over. Zanny's head swam. Her stomach churned, then heaved. It wasn't a burglar lying dead on the living room floor. It was her father.

"No," Zanny screamed. "NO!"

Chapter Three

Zanny sat on a brown tweed sofa in Mrs. Finster's living room the next morning, her hands wrapped around a mug of over-sugared, over-milked tea that she didn't really want. She felt almost numb as a single thought turned over and over in her mind: her father was dead. She still hadn't absorbed what that meant. She knew he had been taken to the hospital morgue — she had seen his body loaded into the ambulance — but she still couldn't believe he was gone forever. She knew that her house now stood empty, but she couldn't take in that it would never again be filled with her father's presence. The mug of tea grew cool in her hands.

In Mrs. Finster's kitchen, Mrs. Finster and Lieutenant Jenkins were speaking in hushed voices.

"Despondent?" Mrs. Finster was saying. "Not that I know of. But that doesn't mean he wasn't. Mitch Dugan wasn't much of a talker. Wasn't much of a mixer, either. He liked to keep pretty much to himself. I can't tell you the number of times I invited him over for my brisket — I'm quite famous for my brisket, you know — and he turned me down every time. Are you married, Lieutenant?"

"Yes, I am," Lieutenant Jenkins said. "Mrs. Finster, when was the last time you spoke with Mitch Dugan?"

"Well, I'm not sure," Mrs. Finster said thoughtfully. "It must have been a few days ago. Thursday, I think. Yes, that was it. I was just coming back from town when I ran into him. He was on his way to work. He was an orderly at the health centre, you know. He sometimes worked the afternoon shift."

"Did you speak to him?"

"I said hello. I always say hello whenever I run into a neighbour. He said hello back."

"How did he seem?"

"Seem?"

"Did he appear to be in good spirits?"

"Good spirits?" Mrs. Finster sounded baffled. There was a moment of silence. Finally, she said, "Well, I can't say. What are you getting at, Lieutenant?"

Zanny knew exactly what he was getting at. She understood what he was trying to get Mrs. Finster to say. Anger surged through her. She set the mug of tea roughly on the table and stood up. She reached the kitchen before Mrs. Finster had the chance to speak again.

"You're wrong," she said. "That's not the way it happened. My father wasn't that kind of person."

Lieutenant Jenkins looked at her with cool grey eyes. "Zanny . . . " he began.

Mrs. Finster frowned. "I'm afraid I don't . . . " Then realization flickered in her eyes. "Oh," she said. "Oh. You think . . . "

"My father didn't kill himself," Zanny insisted "That isn't the way it happened."

Mrs. Finster stood up and came toward her. "Poor child," she said. "You must be hungry. Let me get you something to eat."

But Zanny barely heard her. She was conscious of nothing else in the room except Lieutenant Jenkins.

"You're wrong," she repeated.

"I know how hard this must be for you, Zanny," Lieutenant Jenkins said softly. "But the facts are the facts."

"My father died of a gunshot wound. You told me so yourself. That proves he couldn't have killed himself. My father didn't own a gun."

"I'm afraid he did," Lieutenant Jenkins countered.

His calm voice only angered Zanny more. "You've obviously made a mistake," she said stiffly. "I know my father. And I know he didn't own a gun. He was a hospital orderly."

"I understand how you must feel, Zanny," Lieutenant Jenkins said.

"No you don't. You don't understand at all."

The lieutenant nodded, as if conceding her point. "But the thing is, Zanny, we found two boxes of bullets in your father's bedside table. And we found a holster for the gun in the same drawer."

Zanny stared at him, dumbfounded. Since when had her father owned a gun? What on earth could have possessed him to acquire one? The bullets and the holster must have been planted. Maybe whoever had killed him had tried to make it look like suicide. But who would have wanted to kill her father? No burglar would have gone to all that trouble. But if it wasn't a burglar, then who? Who would have wanted to kill him badly enough to plan such a thing?

"There were only a couple of fingerprints on the gun that killed him, Zanny," Lieutenant Jenkins said, "and they belonged to your father. And there were powder burns on his hand. I know this must be hard to accept, Zanny. I can understand why you wouldn't want to believe it. But the thing is, the coroner has concluded that the injuries your father sustained are consistent with a self-inflicted wound."

All feeling drained from Zanny. From across a great distance she heard muffled words. Heard them, but barely absorbed them.

"Mrs. Finster tells me you have no living relatives," Lieutenant Jenkins said. "Is that true, Zanny?"

Her father had killed himself. No. No, it couldn't be. Her father would never have done that. He was too strong to do a thing like that. Besides, he would never have abandoned her. Would he?

"Zanny? Do you have any relatives? Anyone who we can call?"

But he *had* killed himself, hadn't he? Lieutenant Jenkins had said as much. One day, without Zanny even knowing it, her father had gone out and bought himself a gun. And one day — today — he had picked up that gun and he had . . .

"No," Zanny said. Her voice was a whisper. "There's no one." No one at all.

"I'll have to call Children's Aid," Lieutenant Jenkins said.

"Oh, no," Mrs. Finster protested. "You can't do that. The poor child has already gone through so much."

"I'm sorry, but . . . "

* * *

Zanny had no idea how she ended up in Mrs. Finster's back bedroom. She was just suddenly there, sitting on the edge of the bed, watching Mrs. Finster flit about, folding back blankets, fluffing pillows, pulling out the little suitcase that Zanny had brought with her last night.

"You shouldn't sleep in your clothes," Mrs. Finster said.

Zanny glanced at the clock on the bedside table. It wasn't even noon.

"I'm not tired," she said.

"Nonsense," said Mrs. Finster. "You're exhausted. You didn't sleep a wink last night." She folded her hand over one of Zanny's. "I heard you, dear. You cried all night, you poor thing. Now you need some rest."

Zanny changed into her pyjamas and climbed into the bed. She lay back against the pillow and closed her eyes. Mrs. Finster was right. Sleep would have been welcome. Sleep would have carried her away. It would have numbed her.

But sleep would not come.

Instead of the sweet blackness of oblivion, her

eyes closed onto a full-colour image of her father's body lying in a pool of black-red blood on the living room floor, his eyes staring sightlessly up at her, the rest of his face slack and expressionless.

Only a few hours ago she had been marching home from school, prepared to blast him, prepared to take a stand against him. She wept as she remembered how she had wished that he would never issue her another order, never again tell her what she could do and couldn't do. Tears rolled down her cheeks and made puddles on her pillow. She had wished that he would never bother her again — and now he never would.

She cried until her pillow was soaked, and then, somehow, she slept.

* * *

Zanny slept around the clock and awoke to the smell of bacon. I hope he's making French toast, too, she thought. Her father made the best French toast she had ever tasted, crisp on the outside, soft and eggy on the inside, and laced with just the right amount of cinnamon. Her mouth watered at the thought of it. Then she opened her eyes and saw that she was lying in a strange bed. She squeezed her eyes shut again and wished she could sleep forever.

She lay there for a while, still and empty except for the ache in her heart. He was gone. Gone. She hated the way people used that word when it wasn't at all what they meant. When people were gone, there was always the chance that they would come back. When they were dead, well, that was another matter. She wiped away the tears that stung her eyes. How could he have done it? And to *her?* He probably hadn't thought about that. As he dug out the gun she hadn't known he owned, and loaded it with the bullets she had never seen, he had probably thought that what he was about to do was something he was doing only to himself. Wrong, Mitch Dugan. You missed the boat again. This was something you did to me, too. To *me,* dammit.

Suddenly Zanny was sobbing uncontrollably. She heard herself gulping for air, then the anguish flooded out of her. Her whole body trembled. She couldn't even stop crying when Mrs. Finster appeared and wrapped her arms around her and rocked her. She felt as if she could cry forever.

* * *

"That's right," Mrs. Finster coaxed. "You eat that right up. There's nothing like a full stomach to ease the pain of living." She slid two more pancakes onto Zanny's plate and passed her the syrup, despite her protests. Zanny stared at the cut-glass jug and thought of the pancakes she had already eaten. Surely this wasn't right. Surely someone in her position shouldn't be gorging herself on Mrs. Finster's feather-light pancakes. Surely food should be the last thing on her mind.

"You have to eat," Mrs. Finster said gently, as if she were reading Zanny's mind. "Bad things happen, Zanny, things that make you sadder than you would ever have imagined. But you still have to eat. You have to go on."

Zanny poured syrup onto her pancakes and ate, more slowly now.

"What's going to happen to me?" she said.

"Where am I going to live?"

Mrs. Finster's kindly smile faltered. She wiped her hands on her apron and sat down at the table across from Zanny.

"Don't you have *any* family, dear? Someone who will be able to look after you? There must be *someone.*"

But there wasn't. There had only been the two of them: Zanny and her father. Her mother had died when she was just a baby. She had never known her grandparents.

"No one at all?" Mrs. Finster shook her head. "It doesn't seem possible that anyone could be so alone in the world."

Zanny felt tears well up in her eyes again.

"Oh, dear," Mrs Finster said. She reached across the table for Zanny's hand. "I didn't mean to upset you. I don't know what gets into me sometimes. I think something and the next thing you know, it pops out of my mouth. It got me into more trouble than I can tell you when I was a girl. I'm sorry."

"It's okay," Zanny said. Suddenly the pancakes were like glue in her mouth. She put down her fork and pushed the plate away.

"Just give me a few minutes to clear away these dishes," Mrs. Finster said. "Then I'll drive you into town. There are so many things we have to take care of. There are arrangements to be made."

Arrangements. The pancakes and syrup turned sour in Zanny's stomach. That was another one of those words people used to make things sound better than they were, to lend them an air of cheeriness.

But Mrs. Finster didn't mean flower arrangements or music arrangements. She meant funeral arrangements.

* * *

"What do you think, Zanny?" Mrs. Finster asked. "I think the oak is very nice. So rich. So nicely lined. I buried Mr. Finster in oak, you know. There were some people in the family, his sister Rose, for example, who thought I should have buried him in mahogany. An enduring wood, Rose told me." Mrs. Finster sniffed. "And why did I need an enduring wood when I had a husband who smoked and drank himself into an early grave, leaving me all alone to raise three small boys? He didn't even have an insurance policy. Can you believe that? I was so angry at him. I thought, how could he leave me alone like that, to raise the boys? Luckily my boys are all so bright. They were able to get scholarships to college. But still, I was so angry." She smiled sheepishly at Zanny. "I'm sorry, dear. I shouldn't be rattling on about Mr. Finster, God rest his soul. I know you don't feel that way about your father. I just get carried away. I start talking and I can't stop."

But Zanny *was* angry at her father. She couldn't remember when she had been angrier. Look at what he had done. He had turned her life upside down. Here it was eleven o'clock on a Wednesday morning, and instead of sitting in front of Nick Mulaney in math class, she was standing in the softly lit showroom of Stroud and Sons Funeral Parlour, trying to decide between oak and mahogany. How could he have done this to her? How?

"Zanny? Zanny, dear, what do you want to do?"

Zanny couldn't answer. She could hardly move. Mrs. Finster touched her hand. "You wait here, dear," she said. "I'll take care of everything. Don't you worry."

* * *

"Is this all you have, dear?" Mrs. Finster said. "Don't you have anything more . . . " She groped for the right word. "More appropriate," she said at last. Zanny knew exactly what she meant — something suitable for a funeral.

While Mrs. Finster worked her way through Zanny's closet, Zanny hovered in the doorway. From where she stood, she could see into her father's bedroom. She almost expected to see his long legs stretched out on the bed where he liked to read in the evenings. She had never seen anyone read as much as her father had — recently, anyway. In the past, he'd never had much use for books. But since coming to Birks Falls, he had stopped his habitual pacing, acquired a library card, and spent most of his evenings reading and listening to classical music.

There were none of her father's sounds in the house now. No music. No soft swoosh of turning pages. There was only the sound of Mrs. Finster working her way through Zanny's closet, clucking over the lack of a dress or a skirt sombre enough for the occasion at hand.

What will happen now? Zanny wondered. Will I ever live here again? This house had become her home; she'd lived in it longer than anywhere else. The emptiness inside her spread until she felt completely hollow. She couldn't stay here alone: she wasn't old enough, had never even thought of what it meant to support herself. What would happen? What would they do about her? And who exactly were *they* who now had the power to make decisions about her life?

"I suppose this will have to do," Mrs. Finster announced from the depths of Zanny's closet.

Zanny wiped her eyes and drew in a deep breath. She turned back to her room to see Mrs. Finster fighting her way out of the closet, holding high a navy blue shirtwaist dress that Zanny had forgotten she owned.

* * *

Zanny put on the navy dress, which was too short in the sleeves and too tight at the collar, and a pair of black pumps, and walked over to the church alone before the funeral. Mrs. Finster didn't argue with her. "I'll be there in half an hour," she said. "Are you sure you'll be all right by yourself for half an hour?"

Zanny nodded, telling herself she would be fine. She hadn't realized how she would feel as she walked through the big doors and looked up the aisle to the front of the church, where the sunlight flooded through the stained glass and formed a brilliant pattern on the white satin lining of the coffin.

The church was empty, and she was glad. No one saw her knees wobble as she walked toward the coffin. No one saw her eyes fill with tears as she drew nearer. No one heard her sob as she stared at her father's motionless body. She had never seen anyone lie so still. She stared for a while at his chest, praying that somehow a miracle would happen, that he would draw a breath and that this nightmare would come to an end.

The longer she stared down at him, the more she realized that her father didn't look like himself any more, except remotely, the way the figures in a wax museum are just enough like their real-life models that you know who they're supposed to be, but never marvel at the likeness. Her father's hands were folded over his chest. What little hair he had was neatly combed back. His cheeks had been brushed with a rouge that was probably supposed to give him a healthy glow, but instead gave him a mask-like appearance. His unruly eyebrows had been tamed in death as they never had been in life.

Not for the first time, Zanny was struck by how little she looked like her father. She didn't bear even a slight resemblance to him. All her life people had remarked on their physical dissimilarity. It used to upset her. "Are you sure that's your daughter, Mitch? Are you sure your old lady didn't have something going with the mailman?" For some reason, people thought that was a real rib-buster of a joke. But not Zanny. When she was very small, it had made her cry.

"Never mind," her father would say. "Plenty of kids don't look like their fathers. Plenty of kids are like you, the image of their mothers. You look just like her, Zanny."

But she had only his word for that. Zanny was twenty months old when her mother died. She didn't remember her mother, couldn't remember her, no matter how hard she tried. And there were no photos to jog her memory.

"Didn't you even have wedding pictures?" Zanny had asked.

"Of course we did," her father said. But the pictures were gone. They'd been burned up. Everything had been burned up in a house fire a few weeks before . . . His eyes would always mist over at that point. His voice would crack. The mere mention of Zanny's mother filled him with such heart-wrenching sadness that Zanny could barely stand to ask him anything more about it.

Now people started to file into the small church. Mrs. Finster appeared at Zanny's elbow, touching her lightly, guiding her to one of the front pews. When Zanny took her seat and looked up again, the casket was closed. A basket of lilies sat on top of it. Zanny bowed her head and wept silently. She looked around only once during the funeral service, and caught a glimpse of Michelle, Sheri and Anna sitting together in a pew near the back. She was surprised to see, a few rows in front of them, Nick Mulaney.

For some reason, when Zanny thought of funerals, she thought of bleak November mornings and grey, grim rain. But on the day of her father's funeral, the sun hung like a golden disc in a shimmering blue sky. The grass in the cemetery was as thick and green as a carpet. It was a day for bike-riding and Frisbees in the park; it was a day for running and hiking and jogging, for football and baseball, for jump rope and swings and slides. Zanny watched her father's coffin being lowered into the ground and wondered whether a sunny day would ever seem beautiful to her again.

One by one, people filed by, each throwing a handful of earth into the grave, and each stopping to take her hand, to squeeze it, to say how sorry they were. Zanny recognized many of the faces: neighbours, teachers, friends. Michelle, Sheri and Anna approached her together.

"We're so sorry," Michelle said. Anna and Sheri nodded sombrely.

"We're leaving tomorrow for the state championships," Anna said. "But if there's anything we can do when we get back, you just say the word."

"Anything," Sheri echoed.

Zanny nodded. She knew that if she said something, she would cry, and, for some reason she couldn't quite fathom, she didn't want to cry in front of the Swim Girls. If Lily were here, it would be different. With Lily, she could cry. But not with these girls. She didn't know them well enough to cry in front of them.

She stood at the graveside long after everyone else gone back to Mrs. Finster's house, where light refreshments were being served. Mrs. Finster had squeezed her arm gently.

"Just a few minutes longer," Zanny had said. "I'll be along soon." She couldn't just walk away. She couldn't just leave him alone like that, without saying goodbye.

She mouthed the word silently. It caught in her throat. This parting wasn't at all what she'd expected. She had always thought the goodbye would come when she went away to college, that she'd be leaving her father in the small brick house at the top of the hill, and then only for a few months at a time:

from the start of a semester until the start of the next holiday, until Thanksgiving, or Christmas. She'd never imagined that their parting would be so final, that she would be walking away for good and would never again see his face smiling at her.

She looked at the place in the ground where her father lay, and she tried to understand what had led him to do it. She berated herself for missing all of the signs. They'd done a unit on suicide in Health Studies last year. There had even been a test on it. Question: Name five Suicide Warning Signs. Answer: Depressed mood, loss of appetite, sleeping more than usual, the sudden giving away of cherished possessions, spending more time than usual alone. She'd studied hard for that test, the way she always did. The warning signs were burned into her memory, for all the good they had done her. She hadn't noticed any of them in her father. She had been so wrapped up in her own life that she had been completely blind to the problems in his.

She had been blind to other things, too. Like the gun. When and how had her father bought a gun? And bullets for it. How had he ended up with powder burns on his hands? Lieutenant Jenkins's words echoed in her ears: "The injuries your father sustained were consistent with a self-inflicted wound." He had killed himself. But why? That was the thing she couldn't understand. *Why* had he done it? And how on earth could she have missed all the signs?

Chapter Four

Zanny sat on an old-fashioned rocking swing at the end of Mrs. Finster's yard in the shade of a bank of cedar trees and wondered if everyone had left Mrs. Finster's house yet. She was surprised by how many people had come. Many of them she didn't know. They were people from the hospital, all of whom seemed genuinely saddened by her father's passing, which only deepened Zanny's sorrow. In so many of the places they had lived, her father had been a loner, completely without friends. But in Birks Falls, he had finally found a home; in Birks Falls, he had finally gathered some friends. But it had all come too late. It hadn't helped him find whatever he had been looking for all these years.

"Zanny?"

She looked through tear-blurred eyes and saw Nick Mulaney standing in the middle of Mrs. Finster's lawn, his hands in the pockets of his jeans.

He smiled tentatively at her and gave a sympathetic shrug.

She was touched by his presence, but at the same time she felt awkward. She was going to cry again, there was no avoiding it, and if there was one thing that always made a bad situation worse for her it was crying in front of someone she barely knew.

Nick took a few steps toward her, then stopped. "Maybe you don't feel like company right now," he said. "If you don't, I'll understand. Just say the word and I'll leave." As he stood waiting for her answer, he looked her directly in the eye, which surprised her. Unlike Sheri and Anna and Michelle, Nick didn't seem ill-at-ease. And although he had offered to go, he didn't seem in any hurry to get away from her.

She hesitated, then said, "I'm probably not very good company right now."

"You don't have to be good company." Nick slipped onto the swing opposite her. "I was really sorry to hear about your dad."

Zanny nodded.

"He must have been quite a guy," Nick said. "There sure were a lot of people at the church."

"I guess," Zanny replied. Her voice was hoarse, her throat tight as she tried to choke back tears. Quite a guy, all right. A guy who had obviously been in a lot of pain. A guy whose problems had been so overwhelming that he had gone out and bought a gun and killed himself. And all without his only daughter even knowing what was going on.

"Zanny?" Nick's eyes were filled with concern. "If you want to talk, you can. I'm here to listen. If

45

you don't want to talk, that's all right, too. It's up to you, okay?"

She nodded and wiped away a tear.

They rocked back and forth in silence for a few minutes. Then, slowly, Zanny said, "I just didn't expect it. Of all the things in the world that could have happened, this was the one I never expected. Even when I came home from school that day, even when I saw the police cars and the ambulance sitting right there in the driveway, I still didn't expect it. I never thought anything could ever happen to my father. Not *my* father." When she thought back, it was like walking through a dream. She saw everything so clearly that she could almost reach out and touch the yellow police tape running across her front door, and yet it all had an unreal quality, as if touching anything at all would make the whole scene fade away. "Even when I realized that someone had been killed, even when I saw a body lying on the floor in the living room, I still didn't expect it to be my *father*."

Nick didn't look away. He peered deep into her eyes and nodded, as if he understood every word.

"My mother died a couple of years ago," he said. "I wasn't there when it happened. She and my dad had been divorced for a while, and I was living with Dad. But, boy, I remember that day. I had just come home from school. The phone was ringing. I picked it up and it was my Aunt Louise, my mother's sister. She said, 'Are you alone, Nick?' I remember thinking what a funny question it was. I hadn't talked to my aunt in maybe six months, and the first thing she said was 'Are you alone?' Why would she ask me that?" He paused and drew in a deep breath. "So I told her, 'Yeah, I'm alone.' Dad was still at work. Then she said, 'There's been an accident, Nick. Your mother's been killed.' And you know what I said?"

Zanny shook her head. She could see that he was reliving the moment and suddenly wanted to touch him, to comfort him.

"I said, 'You're kidding.' Dumb, eh? Someone tells me my mother had just died, and the only thing I can say is, 'You're kidding.' " He shook his head again.

"I'm sorry," she said.

Nick's smile was tinged with sadness. "Thanks. But I didn't tell you that to get your sympathy. It's just that, well, some things you never forget, Zanny. Some moments stay with you forever. You live them over and over again. Sometimes it feels like the hurt will never go away, and, in a way, it never does. I know it isn't easy. Boy, do I know."

She nodded. They sat on the swing in silence for a little while. Then she looked into his dark brown eyes, until, puzzled, he frowned.

"Do you know . . . did you hear what happened?" Zanny asked.

"I heard what people are saying, that there was a gun involved. A guy at school told me that someone told him your dad surprised a burglar. You hear about that happening all the time. Someone comes home, there's a burglar in the house, and by the time the guy even knows there's anything wrong — well, you know."

Zanny looked down at the hands knotted in her

lap and almost wished that was what had happened. "The police . . . they say he did it himself." Why was it so hard to say out loud? "They say he killed himself." She wondered how Nick would react. She wondered how she would respond if someone told her the same thing.

He said, "I'm sorry. I'm really sorry."

Somehow the silence that followed wasn't awkward. After a few moments, Nick offered her a gentle smile. "So what happens now? Are you going to go live with relatives somewhere?"

"Not exactly," Zanny said. "I don't have any relatives."

"No relatives?" Nick looked as surprised as everyone always did. "I thought everybody had relatives."

"I don't."

"None at all?"

"None."

"And I thought I was the only person in the world who could hold a family reunion in a phone booth."

"What?" Zanny said in surprise.

"There's me," he said, ticking off his index finger, "and my dad, and Aunt Louise, and that's it. That's every scrap of family I have."

"That's two more relatives than I have," Zanny said grimly.

Nick reached out and took one of her hands in his. His hands were warm and dry. They made her feel safe.

"So what are you going to do?"

Zanny bit her lip. Don't cry, she told herself.

There had been enough tears for one day. "I don't know."

They sat in silence, swinging gently. How could this have happened to her? How could she have *let* it happen? And how could she have missed the warning signs? She couldn't stop thinking about that.

The thing was, though, there had been no signs. There had been nothing out of the ordinary about her father's behaviour, nothing different about his mood. And she simply couldn't imagine her father . . . doing it. She couldn't even imagine him feeling whatever it was a person felt pulling out a gun and — she flinched — putting it to his head . . .

"He didn't do it," she said. It was that simple. "My father didn't do it. He *couldn't* have." She stood up abruptly and got off the swing. "I have to go, Nick."

"Go where? Are you okay, Zanny?"

"I'm fine. I have to go to the police station. I have to talk to Lieutenant Jenkins."

"I'll drive you," Nick said.

Zanny had passed by the Birks Falls police station hundreds of times, but she had never actually been inside. It wasn't at all what she expected. For one thing, it was so small, a squat, red-brick, two-storey building at one end of the main street, next to the Texaco station and across from the bank. It was busier, too, than she had imagined a small-town police station would be. The small office was crowded with people, and the half-dozen phones all seemed to be ringing at the same time. No one noticed when Zanny and Nick stepped in.

Zanny glanced around and spotted Lieutenant Jenkins in a little glassed-in office in one corner of the building. She headed toward him. Nick trotted along behind her.

Lieutenant Jenkins was on the phone, but he glanced up and waved them into the office. Only when she was inside did Zanny notice that someone else was in the room with him. A dark-eyed man in a black overcoat was sitting beside the four-drawer filing cabinet.

Lieutenant Jenkins hung up the phone. "Zanny, this is a surprise," he said. "What can I do for you?"

"I wanted to tell you . . . he didn't do it."

Lieutenant Jenkins frowned. "I'm afraid I don't . . . ."

"My father," Zanny said. "He didn't kill himself. He couldn't have. My father wasn't that kind of person. He could never have done something like that."

The phone on Lieutenant Jenkin's desk rang. Jenkins picked it up and growled his name into the receiver. Then he listened intently. "Yeah," he said finally. "Give me five minutes. I'll be right there." The receiver clicked back into its cradle. "A little girl is missing," he explained, grim-faced. "Someone saw her get into a car." He massaged his temples, looking the way her father sometimes did when he came home from work. "Listen, Zanny, I know how you must feel. But officially, we're still treating it as a suicide . . . "

"What do you mean, 'officially'?" Nick asked.

Lieutenant Jenkins looked at him. "And you are . . . ?"

"Nick Mulaney," Zanny said. "He's a friend of mine. What *do* you mean?"

"I mean, officially, for anyone who wants to know. Unofficially, well . . . " He looked at the other man in his office. "It's funny you showed up here when you did, Zanny. I was just about to tell Special Agent Wiley where he could find you."

The man beside the filing cabinet rose. He was a big man. Extended to full height, he seemed to fill the room.

"Special Agent Wiley is with the DEA," Lieutenant Jenkins said. "The Drug Enforcement Administration. He'd like to talk to you."

The DEA? Zanny looked at Nick. What was going on? What was Lieutenant Jenkins talking about?

"I'd like to speak with Miss Dugan alone, if you don't mind," Special Agent Wiley said. His voice was as deep as rolling thunder.

"No problem," Lieutenant Jenkins said. He grabbed his jacket from a coat rack and shrugged into it. "Come on, son," he said to Nick. "You can wait outside."

Nick hesitated. His look seemed to ask, Are you sure? Zanny nodded. She watched him claim some space on a bench in the outer office.

"Won't you have a seat, Miss Dugan?" Wiley gestured toward the chair he had just vacated.

Zanny shook her head. "I'd rather stand."

Wiley shrugged. "Suit yourself." He circled Lieutenant Jenkins's desk and sat in his chair. "I'd like to ask you a few questions about your father."

Zanny was momentarily confused. What could

the DEA possibly want to know about her father? He was a hospital orderly, not a big international drug dealer or a criminal.

"I think you must have him confused with someone else," Zanny said.

Wiley leaned back in the chair and laced his fingers together into a small tent, regarding her gravely.

"Suppose you let me be the judge of that. I understand your father worked as an orderly in the hospital here in town, that he's been there for the past eighteen months. What did he do before that?"

The question threw Zanny off balance. If Special Agent Wiley knew that her father worked at the hospital as an orderly, and that he had been for a year and a half, then he must have access to her father's employment records. He didn't need her to tell him where her father had worked before.

Wiley watched her for a few moments. Finally he said, "What's the matter, Zanny? Don't you know?"

"Yes, but . . ."

"According to the hospital, when your father applied for the job, he told them that he had last worked on the maintenance staff of a private hospital in Dallas, which has since apparently gone out of business. Before that, he was a maintenance man for a private school in Phoenix, which apparently burned to the ground shortly after your father left."

Zanny frowned. That wasn't right. It wasn't right at all.

"What's the matter, Zanny? Do I have it wrong? Because according to Human Resources at the hospital, that's the information your father gave them when he applied for his job."

Zanny shook her head. Her father would never give out false information. This man was lying to her. But why?

"What do you want?" Zanny demanded.

Wiley leaned back in his chair. "What did your father do in his spare time? Did he have any hobbies, maybe some *expensive* ones? Did he like to take you shopping? Did he give you a good allowance? A pretty girl like you, I bet you have a closetful of clothes at home, isn't that right?"

Zanny shook her head. This man wasn't just confusing her, he was scaring her. She didn't understand his questions. She didn't understand why he was saying things that weren't true. "I don't know what you're talking about."

"Don't you, Zanny? Are you sure?"

His black eyes drilled into her, scaring her even more. Then, slowly, Wiley nodded. "You really don't know, do you." He sighed. "Okay, Zanny, that's all for now."

"I want to know why you're here. What do you want with my father?"

Special Agent Wiley stood up and strode to the door. He opened it for her.

"Thank you for your time, Zanny," he said. "My sympathies on your loss."

Zanny hesitated. She wanted to know, but he clearly wasn't going to tell her. His dark eyes were impenetrable. Reluctantly, she left Lieutenant Jenkins's office. Nick rose to meet her. He frowned.

"Are you all right? What was that all about?"

Zanny didn't answer. She just kept walking. She needed to get out of this place and away from Special Agent Wiley.

"What did that guy want?" Nick asked again when they were in the car.

"I don't know."

"A guy from the DEA wants to talk to you and you don't know why? Come on, Zanny, that doesn't make any sense. He must have said what he wanted."

"Well, he didn't," Zanny snapped. "He didn't say a thing, okay?" She was angry and confused. And scared. How could this be happening? How could her life have changed so much, and so quickly?

Nick shoved the key into the ignition and started the engine. "I'm sorry," he said. "I didn't mean to pressure you. I'll take you home. You look exhausted."

She nodded gratefully. Nick was another change in her life, but a change for the better. "I'm sorry, Nick. I guess I'm not very good company."

He smiled gently at her. "Under the circumstances, you don't have to be good company. And I don't have to be a jerk."

* * *

Zanny lay awake in Mrs. Finster's dentist son's old bedroom and wondered what reason her father could have had for lying about working in Dallas, and then in Phoenix. He must have lied. How else could the hospital have gotten the idea that he had worked in those places? But why?

All the possible answers scared her. Suppose

her father had been hiding out from federal agents, from the DEA. Couldn't that explain why they'd moved around so much, over such a long period of time? Her father had always said it was because he had been laid off from a job, or because he wanted to take advantage of a better opportunity somewhere else. Zanny had always been angry or disappointed to discover that those opportunities were never in the same city, rarely even in the same state. But that was all she had been — angry and disappointed that his job or lack of one meant that they had to move again, and that it never seemed to matter what *she* wanted. He never consulted her. But she had never thought more about it than that — until now.

Zanny stared at the walls, then at the bookcase still filled with textbooks, an encyclopedia, a dictionary, an atlas. She got up from the bed and pulled the atlas from the shelf. She carried it back to the bed and opened it to a full-page map of the United States. She found Newark, New Jersey. Then Phoenix, Arizona. Then Cincinnati, Ohio. Then Los Angeles. As she moved her finger from place to place, she realized that every time they had moved, they had moved hundreds of miles — never less than five hundred, according to the map. As she stared at the atlas, she marvelled that she had never questioned it before. Surely most people didn't move like that, so often and so far away. Surely most people, when they did move, kept in touch with somebody in the place they had just left, even if it was only *one* somebody, and even if it was just for a while, just until they made new friends.

Which raised a completely different point, the

point about friends. They had stopped moving a year and a half ago. They had lived in the same house for a year and a half, and yet nobody came to the house other than her own friends and, except for Lily, none of them liked to stay very long. The way Zanny's father watched them made them nervous. She would have been nervous if some strange man scrutinized her the way her father scrutinized her friends. But she hadn't thought of him as some strange man. He was just her overprotective father. He was so overprotective that he embarrassed her and made her angry. At least, that had always struck her as the main problem with the way he acted. Now it occurred to her that overprotectiveness was only one possible interpretation of the facts.

And that wasn't all. Zanny had always seen her father as a loner, someone who liked to keep to himself when he wasn't working. Now it turned out that he had plenty of friends in Birks Falls, but for some reason he had never invited them home. She thought back to the reception after the funeral. She had been so tired, so numbed, so drained. She heard the people around her talking, some of them spoke directly to her, but the best she had been able to offer in return was a weak smile. So many people she had never met were there. Their names meant nothing when Mrs. Finster repeated them in her ear. But she'd nodded when they spoke to her and she'd smiled because it was polite to smile. There had been one man in particular, a sandy-haired man with red-rimmed blue eyes. Edward something, Mrs. Finster had said. Edward Hunter. Then Mrs. Finster had drifted away to greet someone else.

As the sandy-haired man spoke, tears gathered in his eyes. "I worked with Mitch," he said. He wasn't looking at Zanny. He was staring down at the cup of tea in his hand. "We were best friends."

Zanny gazed at the man dully as he continued to talk. Her head ached. Her eyes burned with fatigue and with the tears she had shed. She had fleetingly tried to imagine her father as someone's best friend, and then Mrs. Finster had brought someone else over to meet her, and Edward Hunter had faded into the background.

Now she thought about it again. How could Edward Hunter claim to be her father's best friend, when she had never heard his name before? Why wouldn't her father have mentioned his name? Why hadn't he ever invited Edward Hunter home to dinner? Was he trying to hide something? And, if so, did it have anything to do with Special Agent Wiley's questions?

Zanny slept only fitfully, and woke with a headache and no appetite for the plate of scrambled eggs Mrs. Finster set in front of her.

"I understand how you feel, dear," Mrs. Finster said. "I couldn't eat for a month after Mr. Finster died. I looked like a skeleton. I lost my strength and almost ended up in the hospital. If it hadn't been for my three boys, I don't know what would have happened to me. They made me see how much I was needed."

Zanny nodded and forced down a forkful of egg, but only because she didn't want to appear rude. If it wasn't for Mrs. Finster, Zanny didn't know where she would be right now. The fact was, no one needed

Zanny. No one would care if she starved herself or ended up in the hospital.

After she cleared away the breakfast dishes, Mrs. Finster drove Zanny to an office above a shoe store on the town's main street.

"I'll be at the bakery," Mrs. Finster said. "My dear friend Rose runs it. She sent over those little sweet buns everyone seemed to enjoy so much yesterday. You come and find me there when you've finished."

Zanny nodded and climbed up the stairs to a long hallway. She took moment to orient herself. Then she found the door she was looking for: William Sullivan, Attorney.

Mr. Sullivan himself greeted her at the door. He was a grey-haired man with a deeply lined face and lively blue eyes. He grasped her hand firmly, shook it and said, "I'm pleased to meet you, Alexandra. I'm just sorry it had to be under these circumstances I'm sorry about what happened to your father. He was a fine man." He smiled pleasantly at her. "Can I get you anything? A cup of tea, perhaps?"

"No, thank you."

"Well then, why don't we just go into my office and get down to business. I know the reading of a will isn't something most people look forward to, but it has to be done. The loose ends have to be tied up. What do you say, Alexandra?"

Zanny nodded. Just as she started to follow Mr. Sullivan into the inner office, the door from the hall opened. Special Agent Wiley stepped in, brushed by Zanny and flashed his identification at Mr. Sullivan.

"I'm here for the reading of the will," he said.

Mr. Sullivan's pale blue eyes hardened as he read the identification. He looked sternly at Wiley. "In that case, I'd like to see your warrant."

"Your client — *former* client — is under active investigation by my department," Wiley said. "If I have to go through the formality of getting a warrant, I will. But it would be much easier if you just let me sit in on the reading."

"The law wasn't written to make things easy for you, Mr. Wiley," Mr. Sullivan told him. "Produce a warrant and you can stay. No warrant, no will."

Wiley's black eyes bored into the old lawyer.

"Make no mistake about it," he said. "I will get my warrant, and I will see that document."

Mr. Sullivan smiled blandly. "Just so long as everything is legal."

After Wiley had left, Mr. Sullivan turned to Zanny and with perfect composure said, "Shall we?" He didn't seem at all perturbed to have been face to face with a federal agent. Zanny wondered if he had been expecting the visit.

"Do you know what that was all about, Mr. Sullivan?" Zanny asked.

Mr. Sullivan shrugged. "Apparently the authorities have some interest in your father."

"But do you know *why?*"

"No. I don't. Nor do I see why you should be concerned, unless you know of some reason why they should be interested in *you.*"

Horrified, Zanny shook her head.

"I'm sure I'll see Mr. Wiley again," Mr. Sullivan went on. "You may see him, too. If you do, Alexandra, make sure that whatever he wants, he's operating under the proper authority. If you have any doubts, call me. I'd be only too happy to act on your behalf." He fished a business card out of his pocket and handed it to her. "My home phone number is on there, too, in case there's no answer here. Now then," he said, standing aside to usher her into his inner office, "shall we take a look at the will?"

He showed Zanny to a high-backed leather chair and seated himself behind a mahogany desk. He opened one of the desk's drawers and pulled out a thick file folder. Zanny caught a glimpse of the folder's label. It bore her father's name. The lawyer extracted a few sheets of paper, then closed it again.

"Do all those papers have to do with my father?" Zanny asked.

Mr. Sullivan nodded. "I looked after all of your father's legal affairs."

"What kind of legal affairs?"

His smile was enigmatic. "I'm afraid I'm not at liberty to say, my dear. There is the matter of client privilege."

"Meaning?"

"Meaning that what business I took care of for your father is strictly confidential. Please be assured that there is nothing for you to be concerned about. Your father was a prudent man. He took all the steps to ensure that, should anything happen to him, you would be provided for. Now, as to the will. I think the important thing you should know — well, actually, there are two important things — the first is that your father had a substantial paid-up life insurance policy. You won't have to worry about money. The second is that your father made provisions for your care in the event that anything should happen to him."

Her care? "What do you mean?"

"He named a guardian for you."

"He did?" For the life of her Zanny couldn't imagine who he would have chosen.

"A Mr. Everett Lloyd of Chicago," Mr. Sullivan said.

It was a name Zanny had never heard before. "Who's he?"

Mr. Sullivan raised an eyebrow. "Not someone you know?"

Zanny shook her head.

"I see." Mr. Sullivan looked surprised. "I've notified the police. They'll locate and contact Mr. Lloyd. Until they do, I don't think there's much point in worrying about the matter. Why don't I just read this to you . . . "

Zanny only half listened as the elderly lawyer read and explained the document. Mostly she wondered who Everett Lloyd was, and why she had never heard the name of the person her father had trusted enough to be responsible for the care of his only daughter. Did Everett Lloyd have anything to do with the DEA? Did he have anything to do with why the DEA was so interested in her father? She wondered, too, what other legal affairs Mr. Sullivan had handled for her father, and why he had reacted to the presence of a federal agent in his office as if it were an everyday occurrence.

* * *

After she left Mr. Sullivan's office, Zanny walked to the bakery in a daze. Mrs. Finster got up from one of the small tables where she had been drinking tea and hurried over.

"My dear, are you all right?" she said. "You look so pale."

"I want to go to the hospital."

The older woman looked alarmed. "Why? You aren't ill, are you?"

"N . . . no." She hadn't even known that the words were going to come out of her mouth. In fact, until just now she'd had no idea that she wanted to visit the hospital. It had just come to her, like a vision. She had been walking across the street, thinking about her father and about the funeral and about Everett Lloyd, whom she had never heard of, and Edward Hunter, the best friend that she had just recently heard of, when suddenly she knew she had to go to the hospital. She had to talk to Edward Hunter. "I just . . . " Just what? "I just wanted to see where he . . . where my father worked."

The concern faded from Mrs. Finster's face. She nodded. "I understand, dear," she said. "I'll drive you there if you'd like."

Zanny nodded gratefully. It was a long way to the hospital. But she didn't want to be an inconvenience, so when Mrs. Finster dropped her off, Zanny said, "I'll take the bus back."

"Take as long as you need, dear. I'll have supper waiting when you get home."

As she walked through the main doors of the large regional hospital, Zanny tried to remember her brief conversation with Edward Hunter.

"No, I'm not a doctor," he had said. "I'm a medical librarian."

She asked the harried nurse at the admitting desk where the library was. It was on the top floor of the hospital's oldest wing, a wing that looked like it was in the process of being either renovated or condemned. The two floors immediately below it were shrouded in drop-cloths and spidered with scaffolding. As she peeked through the glass in the doors, Zanny noted the eerie quiet of those floors; they seemed dead compared to the bustling scene she had left behind in Admitting. Uncertainly, Zanny climbed the last flight of stairs, following the nurse's instructions. Maybe she had misunderstood. Maybe she had taken a wrong turn.

Then, at the very top of the stairs, she saw a small sign: Library. Next to it, an arrow pointed to a door. Zanny pushed it open and walked slowly down a well-lit but deserted corridor. Then, suddenly, there she was, at the entrance of a spacious, sun-drenched library. People, most of them in white coats, were dotted at the tables; a woman sat in front of a computer terminal at the main counter. Zanny walked toward her.

"Excuse me," she said. "I'm looking for the librarian."

The woman smiled pleasantly at Zanny. "I'm the librarian. I'm Mary Letourneau."

Zanny shook her head. "I'm looking for Edward Hunter."

"I'm afraid Mr. Hunter doesn't work here any more," Mary Letourneau said. "He left a few weeks ago."

"Do you know where I can find him?"

"He left to start a hospice."

"A hospice?"

"A place for children who are . . . seriously ill. He bought that old house down on River Street." She reached for a Rolodex and started to flip through it. "I'm sure I can find the address for you. Unless . . . " She paused. "Is there something I can help you with?"

"My father used to work here," Zanny said. "Not *here,* not in the library. He was . . . an orderly." She had to struggle to say the word. This woman wouldn't know him. She was a librarian. What would a librarian know about an orderly?

The woman frowned a little. "You're Mitch Dugan's daughter, aren't you?" Zanny nodded. "I was very sorry to hear what happened. Mitch used to come up here a lot, you know. I think he spent almost all of his lunch hours up there." She pointed upward.

Zanny looked up and saw the skylight that filled most of the ceiling. A gallery ran along three sides of the library. It was filled with shelves of books.

"We keep all the old books up there," Mary Letourneau explained. "I guess you could call it our archives. Your father liked to go up there. To that corner, mostly." She pointed to the middle gallery, where the sunlight was brightest. "He liked to sit up there at lunch time and just quietly read."

Zanny wondered what drew him up there. She tried to imagine her father climbing the spiral staircase every day and sitting there, alone.

"May I?" Zanny asked.

The librarian smiled. "Sure. Go ahead." Then, before Zanny could walk away, she added, "Your father was a really nice man. He liked to keep to himself, mostly. But he always had a kind word. And the kids, of course, loved him."

"The kids?" What was she talking about?

"On Two East. The children's ward. When your father wasn't up there, enjoying the solitude, he was down on Two East. The kids down there really need cheering up, and your father always seemed to know exactly how to do it."

The phone rang. Mary Letourneau reached to answer it. "Take as much time as you like," she said to Zanny.

Zanny climbed the stairs to the middle gallery. From up there, in the flood of sunlight, she could see the whole library below. With the skylight only two metres above her head, she could see the clear blue sky and the treetops on the hills. She knew then why her father liked this place. There was a wonderful peacefulness about it, a comforting tranquillity. She would never have imagined him in such a place. She had never thought much about what he did at work. She had certainly never imagined him spending time on the children's ward.

The librarian had said, "The children down there really need cheering up, and your father knew how to do that." That was something else Zanny couldn't quite picture: her father cheering up a bunch of little children. She decided to pay a visit to the ward, to see another place where he had spent his time.

She made her way down the deserted stairwell and back through the long corridor that connected the west wing with the rest of the hospital.

Two East was sunshine yellow and decorated with enormous cartoon characters in bright reds and greens and blues. One large, colourful room held eight beds; another dozen rooms along the hallway held two beds each. Almost all of them were filled.

"Excuse me," said a voice behind Zanny. "Can I help you?"

Zanny whirled around to face a white-suited nurse who smiled at her from a kindly face. Recognition flickered in her eyes.

"You're Mitch Dugan's daughter, aren't you?" she said. "I saw you at the . . . " Her voice trailed off. She smiled again. "Can I help you with something?"

Zanny stared helplessly at the woman. Suddenly she didn't know what she wanted to say; she had no idea how to explain what had brought her here.

"Your father spent a lot of time up here," the nurse added. "He got along so well with the children."

Once again, Zanny was filled with wonder. At home, her father hardly exchanged hellos with the neighbours. He had turned down dozens of Mrs. Finster's dinner invitations. And now people were saying that this same man, the man she had always thought of as reclusive, spent his spare time with sick children, and had the power to make them laugh.

"I don't know how he did it," the nurse continued. "It was a gift, I guess. There wasn't a child here who he couldn't get to smile. And these kids really need it."

The way she said it made Zanny think about what the librarian had said.

"What do you mean?" Zanny asked. "What's so special about these kids?"

The nurse was silent for a moment. Then she said, "The kids on this ward all have cancer. A lot of them . . . don't go home again."

* * *

The hospital was five kilometres from Mrs. Finster's house. As Zanny walked them, she tried to digest all she had learned about her father. There was so much that remained a mystery, so much she wanted to know but didn't, so much that troubled her. She wished that it were possible to know everything about her father. But the ache in her heart told her that it was far too late.

Chapter Five

"Don't be ridiculous," Mrs. Finster said. "What could be easier than a tuna sandwich? Tuna has plenty of protein. A young girl like you, with all you've been going through, you need protein. You need to stay strong. Sit. Have some juice. I'll just be a minute."

Zanny opened her mouth to protest again, but the telephone rang. Mrs. Finster bustled into the kitchen to answer it.

Zanny reached for her juice. She should have gone to school. She shouldn't have let herself be talked into staying away for a while. Mrs. Finster hovered over her every minute. "Just checking on you, dear," she would say. "Just making sure you have everything you need."

Zanny was grateful that Mrs. Finster had taken her in. She couldn't even imagine where she would be right now if Mrs. Finster hadn't offered her a place to live for a while. *A while.* Zanny wondered how long that would turn out to be. How long would it take for the police to locate the mysterious Everett Lloyd? What would happen if they couldn't find him? She couldn't stay with Mrs. Finster forever. But if not here, where?

She wished she was at school, and at the same time, she felt glad that she wasn't. She had gone to school once with a kid whose father had died. and had seen the way everyone avoided the kid at first. "Did you hear what happened?" they whispered to one another. "His father died of cancer." They steered clear because they didn't know what to say. "What do you say to a kid whose father died?" As if that were the real question, what *they* were supposed to say, instead of how the poor kid was feeling.

So Zanny hadn't gone to school. But she couldn't stay here under Mrs. Finster's ever-watchful eye forever.

She looked out Mrs. Finster's dining room window, across the sweep of her lawn to the hedge of honeysuckle and, beyond that, across a wide expanse of open field to the trim red brick of her own house. If she didn't belong there, and she couldn't stay here, where would she go? Where would she end up? Did the mysterious Everett Lloyd still live in Chicago? Would she have to live with him, assuming he was even interested in looking after her? Was he married? Did he have kids of his own? Was *he* even alive? She stared at her own little house and wondered, What next? What will happen to me next?

A man strode up the driveway toward her house

as if he owned the place. Zanny went to the window for a closer look. It was Special Agent Wiley. What was he doing there? He stopped at the front door and tried the handle. Zanny shook her head. Did he really think she had left the place unlocked?

As she watched, Wiley pulled something from his pocket. She couldn't see right away what it was. Then his actions told her. He had a key. Somehow he had managed to get a key to her house and he was unlocking the door.

Zanny glanced into the kitchen. Mrs. Finster was still on the phone, probably engaged in another interminable conversation with her sister Minnie. The two of them couldn't seem to get through a day without exchanging half a dozen phone calls. Zanny let herself out Mrs. Finster's front door and ran across the field to her own house. Who did he think he was? He couldn't go in her house without permission. He had no right.

Rage carried her up the front steps. As she grasped the handle to push the door open, something crashed inside. Special Agent Wiley had broken something — something that didn't even belong to him. Zanny pushed the door open and stepped inside. Through the door that led to the kitchen, she saw Wiley crouching, picking up shards of the shattered sugar bowl from the floor. His sharp eyes skittered from the job at hand to her the minute she crossed the threshold. He didn't look surprised to see her.

"Well, well, Zanny," he said, straightening. "What are you doing here?"

Zanny's anger reached the boiling point. What

was *she* doing here? The real question was, what was *he* doing here? What gave him the right to charge through her kitchen like a bull in a china shop, breaking her father's things?

Special Agent Wiley followed her eyes to the shattered sugar bowl.

"I'm sorry," he said. "I know you probably won't believe me, but I don't really enjoy this job. I'd rather be out fishing than searching your house."

She regarded him with disdain. "You actually expected to find something in my sugar bowl?"

Wiley shrugged. He looked rather sheepish. "It must look like something out of an old movie."

"A very *bad* old movie," she shot back.

"The fact is, it really is amazing what you find in some people's sugar bowls."

What had he expected to discover? "What does he want with my father?" she had asked Mr. Sullivan. "What could the DEA possibly want with my father?"

"There's only one way to get the answer," Mr. Sullivan had said. "And that's to ask the question."

Zanny had trembled at the thought. Wiley worked for the federal government. How could she ask him? Now, looking into his black eyes, she thought, how can I *not* ask him?

"What do you want?" she demanded. "What are you looking for?"

Wiley picked up the last piece of the sugar bowl and dropped it into the garbage. "You never really know what you're going to find until you start looking."

She didn't believe him. You didn't march into someone's house and start tearing the place apart without any idea of what you were after.

"You'd better tell me what you're looking for, or I'm going to call the police and tell them that I caught you breaking in here."

Special Agent Wiley smiled indulgently. "You can't call the cops on me, Zanny," he said. "I *am* the cops. Look, I know this is your house. I respect that. But I have a job to do. And my best advice to you is to let me do it. If you don't, *I'll* call the cops and have you arrested for obstructing my investigation."

Zanny shook with rage and fear. She wanted him out of her house. More than that, she wanted answers.

"What do you want here? What are you investigating? What do you think my father did?"

"This is a confidential federal investigation. I don't have to tell you a thing. But I am going to tell you, Zanny, because I think you have a right to know."

His acquiescence took her by surprise. Suddenly she wasn't sure she wanted to know.

"Did you ever notice," he asked, "how much you've moved around with your father over the years? You have, haven't you? I bet you've lived in more places than you can remember."

Zanny said nothing. Wiley nodded. "I bet your father didn't make friends easily, either," he said. "And when *you* made friends, I bet he always had a hundred or so questions for them, didn't he?"

Zanny tried to look indifferent. It wasn't easy. He was so sure of himself.

Wiley eyed her appreciatively. "How old are you, Zanny? Fifteen? Sixteen?"

"Sixteen."

"Well, in that case, I bet you and your father did a lot of arguing lately. You're at the age when you want to be out more than you want to be home, when you want to spend more time with your friends. But I bet your father didn't like that very much, did he? Even after all this time, I bet he was still nervous. He wanted to know where you were every minute of every day, and who you were with. I bet he was pretty strict about those curfews, too, wasn't he?"

Zanny went pale with anger and surprise. How did he know so much about her and her father?

"Have you been spying on us?" she demanded.

Wiley shook his head. "Up until a couple of days ago, I didn't even know where you were. In fact, I assumed you must have left the country. I think everyone did."

"Everyone?" What was he talking about? "Who's 'everyone'?" she asked. "What does the DEA want with my father?"

"There were a lot of people at the funeral," Wiley remarked. He had a slow, easy way of talking, as if he were passing a lazy day with an old friend. It made a chilling contrast to what he was saying. "I guess a lot of people must have thought pretty highly of him."

Zanny sensed a trap. "I guess," she said cautiously.

"I wonder what all those nice people would

think if they knew Mitch Dugan wasn't who he pretended to be."

Once more she asked a question without being sure she wanted to know the answer. "What do you mean?"

"I'll tell you what I'm looking for, Zanny. I'm looking for ten million dollars."

"*What?*"

"You heard me. Ten million dollars. The ten million dollars your father stole. You look surprised. Either you're a good actor, or you really didn't know. Your father isn't who you thought he was, Zanny. His name wasn't Mitch Dugan. His real name was Michael Alexander. Your real name is Melissa Alexander. The reason you moved around so much is that your father was on the run — from the government, and from one of the biggest crime families in the country. I hate to be the one to tell you, but the fact is, your father was a crook. A big-time crook."

No. No, it couldn't be. He was mistaken. He either had the wrong person or he was lying. Except that there he was, with his DEA identification and his official-looking badge and the key to her house, which he must have got from the local police, and all those facts. The facts were the worst part. They had really shaken her. He knew how her father thought; he knew things about their private lives that no one else knew.

"It would be in your own best interests to help me recover the stolen money," Wiley continued. "It would also be in your interest to remember that this is strictly confidential. We'd like to keep a low profile on this. We don't want the Pescis to know we found Michael Alexander."

"The Pescis?"

"The bad guys. The crime family your father stole the money from. If they knew your father was here, they'd be all over this place, looking for that money. And that would put *your* life in danger. Those guys wouldn't hesitate to blow you apart if they thought you had any idea where the ten million was hidden."

Zanny stared at him, her insides churning. She didn't like this man: she didn't like what he was telling her.

"You're planning to search this house?" she said, struggling to keep her voice from trembling, but not quite succeeding.

"From top to bottom and every place in between."

He was a federal agent. There seemed to be little Zanny could do except, as Mr. Sullivan had advised, to make sure that he played by the rules.

"I'd like to see your search warrant," Zanny said.

"Do yourself a favour, Zanny. Run along and let me do my job."

Zanny held her ground. "I'd like to see your warrant, please," she repeated. "I know you can't just barge into a private home and tear it apart without some kind of authorization."

"Look, I understand how you feel. . . . " The barbed irritation in his voice made Zanny feel good. It gave her courage.

"Either you produce a warrant, Mr. Wiley, or

I'm calling the police. Just because you're some kind of cop yourself, that doesn't mean you don't have to obey the law."

Wiley glowered at her. Zanny dug into her jeans pocket for the card William Sullivan had given her. She started toward the phone.

"Look, kid, I have nothing personal against your father. I just want to get my job done and then get out of here."

Zanny picked up the telephone receiver and began to dial. Wiley watched her. By the time she had dialled three numbers, he was shaking his head in surrender.

"Okay," he said. "Okay. But you're kidding yourself if you think I won't get that warrant. And you're kidding yourself if you think I won't be back. I have a job to do, and I intend to do it."

Zanny trembled as she watched him walk from the house.

Chapter Six

"Such a nice-looking boy," Mrs. Finster said. She smiled over Zanny's shoulder at Nick standing in the front hall. "Did your father approve of him?"

Zanny looked at Nick and wondered what her father would have thought.

"He never met Nick."

"I see," Mrs. Finster said. "Well, he seems like a nice boy. So polite. I didn't know boys were so polite these days. So often you see boys who think it's smart to be rude." She smiled at Nick again. "Did your father have a curfew for you?"

"Nine-thirty," Zanny answered.

"Nine-thirty?" Mrs. Finster seemed surprised. "Well, if that was what your father wanted . . . " She looked at Nick again, and her face softened. "You be home by eleven, Zanny. And you," she said to Nick, "you take good care of her and make sure she's back on time. Eleven o'clock and no later."

Nick nodded. As he and Zanny strolled down Mrs. Finster's walk together, he asked, "So, what are you in the mood for? A movie? Something to eat? Roller-skating?"

"Roller-skating?" For some reason, she couldn't picture Nick on a roller rink.

"It was just a suggestion," he said. He led her to a black Toyota and opened the passenger door for her. As he slid in behind the steering wheel, she said, "Do you really roller-skate?"

He shrugged and looked embarrassed. "I'm not exactly up to Olympic standards, if that's what you mean."

"There are no Olympic standards in roller-skating," Zanny said. "It's not an Olympic sport."

"Okay, okay. So it was a dumb idea. I just thought . . . I thought I'd be so bad at it that it might get a laugh out of you. It seems to me you could use a laugh about now."

Zanny was flooded with warmth. He was so sweet. She hadn't known him for long, and yet, of all the people at school, he was the only one who'd come to see her. He was the only one who wasn't afraid to meet her sorrow head on. The Swim Girls were out of town at the swim meet, but Zanny had the feeling that even if they weren't, they wouldn't have rushed over to be with her. They would have felt awkward. After all, they weren't really her friends — not the kind of friends that mattered, anyway. She wondered what Nick would say when she told him what she really wanted to do tonight. There was only one way to find out.

"Nick?"

He looked at her with his sweet chocolate eyes.

"Nick, do you think we could go to the library?"

"The library?" He sounded surprised, "Jeez, Zanny, I know exams are coming up, but the library? I thought maybe we could have a little fun."

"It's important, Nick. I want to find something." She had been thinking about what Special Agent Wiley had said. She didn't want to believe him; in fact, she wanted to prove him wrong. She had thought about her father, and the strange way he had led his life. She wanted so badly to believe there was some rational explanation for that, an explanation that had nothing to do with ten million dollars. She had come up with only one way to try to get at the truth. "They keep old newspapers at the library, don't they?"

"I think so, yeah." Nick frowned. "Why? Are you working on a history project or something?"

Zanny hesitated. Wiley had warned her not to talk to anyone. Even if he hadn't, she wasn't sure she was ready to tell anyone what he had revealed. Besides, who knew if she would find what she was looking for?

"If you don't want to take me to the library, it's okay," she said, reaching for the door handle. "But I have to go there, and the sooner, the better. Look, I'm not very good company right now anyway. Why don't I just go? Maybe I could call you tomorrow, okay?" She opened the car door.

Nick reached across her, startling her with the suddenness of his move, and pulled the door shut again.

"If you want to go to the library, we'll go. History was never my best subject, but for you, anything."

Zanny smiled as Nick turned the key in the ignition.

* * *

With help from the reference librarian, Zanny located shelves of thick bound newspaper indexes and a wall of cabinets with thin drawers. Each drawer was filled with dozens of spools of microfilm; each spool contained dozens of issues of newspapers.

"The microfilm readers are over there," the librarian said. "If you find anything you'd like to make a copy of, we have a microfilm copier. The instructions are taped to the wall beside it. If you need any help, just come and find me."

Zanny nodded without taking her eyes off the drawers. There were hundreds of them. Who would have thought the public library in a town this size would have so many newspapers?

"Quite a collection, isn't it?" the librarian said proudly. "Anderson Bently was born here. He's the publisher of one of the biggest newspaper chains in the country. Mr. Bently believes that newspapers are the recorders of society, the on-the-spot historians. He endowed this library quite generously with that history. We have one of the finest collections of Bently newspapers in the state. If you start with the indexes, I'm sure you'll have no trouble finding whatever you're looking for. Unless you're looking for something that goes back further than ten years." The librarian smiled. "Unfortunately, no one ever explained the benefits of indexing to Mr. Bently. His grandson started the indexes after Mr. Bently died, but there was no provision for funding to index retroactively."

"What happens if we want to search back further than ten years?" Zanny asked.

"You'll have to go directly to the microfilm," the librarian replied. "As long as you know the year and the month, you should have no trouble."

After the librarian had gone, Nick said, "Exactly what *are* we looking for?"

Zanny stared at the bank of drawers. "I'm not sure." She hadn't thought it through all the way. "If someone stole, say, ten million dollars, would that be a big deal? I mean, do you think we'd hear about it?"

"We? You mean, you and me?"

"I mean, would it be on the news? Would we read about it in the newspaper?"

Nick looked baffled. "If a guy stole ten million dollars? Any guy in particular?"

She shook her head impatiently. "If a man stole ten million dollars, would you and I see it in the newspaper?" She didn't know how to make the question any clearer.

"Well, yeah," he said slowly. He still looked confused. "Yeah, I guess."

"If a man lived in *this* state and did that, do you think it would be in the papers here?"

"Ten million? Sure, I guess. That's a lot of money."

"What about it if happened in another state?"

"What?"

Because if it had happened, that was probably how it had happened. Her father wouldn't have moved them around so much only to end up back in the same state where he had committed the crime —

if, in fact, he had committed a crime.

"If a guy stole ten million in another state, would we read about it here?"

"Yeah, I guess. Zanny, are you going to tell me what's going on?"

It was a lot of money. Especially since it had happened such a long time ago. But how long ago, exactly? She and her father had been moving around for as long as she could remember, which meant that it must have happened before she could remember. Or maybe they had always moved around a lot, and it had happened without her even noticing it — if, she reminded herself, it had happened at all. So it could have been any time within the past fifteen or sixteen years. She looked at the shelves of indexes and the drawers of microfilm, and then at Nick.

"Will you help me?" she asked.

He nodded without hesitation. "I don't know why. I don't even know what you're looking for. But, sure, I'll help you."

"I'll explain, I promise I will. But not now. Later, okay?"

"Okay," Nick said.

She was filled with gratitude. "The indexes aren't going to help us," Zanny said. "What we're looking for happened fourteen or fifteen years ago. We'll have to look at the microfilm. Why don't you take the West Coast papers? I'll take East Coast."

He peered at the drawers until he found the one he needed, then walked over and yanked it open. "What exactly are we looking for?"

"Anything we can find about a ten-million-dollar robbery."

Nick nodded and carried a few spools to one of the microfilm readers. What must he think, Zanny wondered. Probably that I'm a lunatic. He hardly knew her, they were on their very first date — well, it was the first time they had gone out together, just the two of them — and where had she dragged him? To the public library, blathering all the way about ten-million-dollar robberies. He must think she was crazy, and yet here he was, threading a spool of microfilm into a reader, ready, willing and able to do what she wanted him to do. Which meant that either he was the sweetest person in the whole world, or that there was something seriously wrong with him.

"Nick?"

He glanced up and smiled at her.

"I really appreciate this."

They worked side by side, cranking spool after spool of film across their reading screens. Zanny was surprised at the number of familiar stories she passed, things she had heard her father talk about and that she had always considered ancient history. She would have loved to read them but she couldn't let herself stop, not if she was going to work her way through as many spools as possible before the library closed. She only had time to skim the headlines. After she had finished the first spool and loaded a second, she no longer read all of those. By then she knew exactly which sections of the newspaper carried the kind of story she was looking for, and which sections were a waste of time. She finished the second spool in half the time, and noted with satisfaction that Nick was keeping pace with her.

"I haven't seen anything yet that even comes close to a ten-million-dollar heist," he said. "But I did see a million-dollar bank truck hold-up — in Texas. It wasn't a big story, but it was there. So I guess if I'm reading about a million-dollar job that happened that far away, for sure I'll see one for ten million if it's there." He smiled as he looked back at the screen and began to crank through another spool.

Zanny watched him for a moment, grateful for his help. She couldn't believe she had been lucky enough to find him. She returned to her own work, a little more buoyed, a little more hopeful that she really might be able to discover something that would prove Wiley wrong. Side by side, they read in silence. After a time, a voice called softly to them from the door to the room.

"Ten minutes," the librarian said. "We close in ten minutes."

Ten minutes. It wasn't much time, not nearly enough. Zanny cranked the handle a little faster, skipping another business section, another sports section, another fashion section.

Nick stretched in his chair. "We can always come back tomorrow. I don't mind. We could come here first thing in the morning and spend the day here."

"What about school?"

He shrugged. "What about it? What's more important, Zanny? This, or school?"

"I don't want to get you into trouble with your father."

"What he doesn't know won't hurt me. What do you say, do we have a date?"

She nodded. "But you can meet me here *after* school," she said. "I don't want you ditching classes on my account, Nick."

"But . . ."

"It looks like this is going to take longer than I thought. After school, okay?"

He sighed and nodded. "Okay. After school it is." He got up. "I'll be back in a minute. I have to, uh, use the facilities." Before he left, he bent and kissed her lightly on the cheek.

Zanny's heart sang as she watched him walk away. The memory of his lips electrified her. They were so soft, so warm. She smiled as she turned to unload her own spool of microfilm. Then she thought, I could cover a few more days while I wait for him.

She stumbled on it almost immediately, and when she did, she almost passed right by it. The article wasn't a long one, but it wasn't short either. A picture accompanied it. She read the story quickly, and looked at the photo. Then she zipped forward to the next day's paper, and the next, and the next. Nothing. She couldn't find another word about the incident.

She looked around. Nick still hadn't returned. Quickly, she pulled out the spool, carried it over to the only microfilm copier, and slipped it onto the machine's spindles. As she dug in her purse for some coins she looked at the photo displayed on the screen. Then she dropped the coins into the slot and pushed a button. Almost instantly she had a paper copy.

Behind her, she heard approaching footsteps. Nick.

Zanny folded the paper quickly, not even sure why she was doing it, except that she knew this was something she wasn't ready to share with anyone, not even Nick, not yet. She tucked the folded sheet of paper into her purse and quickly pulled the spools from the copier. She finished winding them by hand, and was tucking the rewound spool into its box when Nick reached her.

"Ready to go?" he asked.

She nodded.

Instead of going straight back to Mrs. Finster's, they stopped at a coffee and dessert place Nick knew. Zanny wasn't sure how it happened, but she started talking about her father, mostly about all the good things she remembered. He had been an odd father, but not a bad one, and suddenly it seemed important for Nick to know this. She even told him how, when she was feeling down after yet another first day at yet another new school, her father would wrap his arms around her and say, "You can do it, Teddy." That was his pet name for her, because of a little birthmark on her bottom. She blushed whenever her father mentioned it. "It looks just like a teddy bear," he said. "At least, it did when you were a baby. We always called you Teddy back then. You were our little teddy bear."

Talking about it felt good. Then, suddenly, as if a big hand had reached inside her and flipped a switch, Zanny felt sad. Her father was gone. Really gone. He was never coming back. This couldn't really have happened to her. She couldn't be so completely alone. It couldn't be that she would never see him again. It just couldn't be. She started to cry. Nick gave her some tissues, held her hand and, as promised, returned her to Mrs. Finster's just before eleven.

"So I guess I'll see you tomorrow then," he said as he left her at the door. "How about I swing by and pick you up here instead of meeting you there?"

Zanny frowned. There?

"The library," Nick said. "I thought you wanted to go back to the library tomorrow."

She'd forgotten. She'd made that arrangement before she'd found what she was looking for.

"I've changed my mind," she said. "I don't want to go back."

Nick looked baffled, but he didn't argue with her.

* * *

Zanny sat cross-legged on the bed and frowned at the hairbrush on the dresser. She remembered the morning her father had stared at his own brush, examining the strands of hair caught in it. He'd bent and twisted every which way to get a glimpse of the back of his head. Finally he had sent her to find a hand mirror and managed to locate what Zanny had noticed some time before — a thinning patch of hair at the back of his head.

"Looks like your old man is losing it," he said. He didn't react at all the way she'd expected. On TV, men were always depressed about losing their hair.

None of them smiled when they discovered those sparse areas on top. But her father seemed pleased by the prospect of balding; he seemed to be looking forward to it. And he had grown into it well. The one time she had broached the subject of a toupee, he had laughed. "Hey, haven't you heard, women find bald men very attractive."

At the time, she'd admired how well he was coping. If she were the one losing her hair, she wouldn't have been nearly so chipper. Now she knew that he had a very good reason for wanting to go bald, for wanting to look different.

She stared down at the copy of the article from the library, and at the picture that accompanied it. She read it again. The words were the same the tenth time as they had been the first. She kept hoping that she had misread, but she hadn't.

It had happened nearly fifteen years ago, in Chicago, half a continent away. A man named Taglia had been killed. A police spokesman speculated that this could be part of some trouble with the Pesci family, which he referred to as an "an alleged crime family." It appeared that some money had been stolen from this "alleged crime family," an amount estimated at ten to twenty million dollars. By any estimate, it was a lot of money, which made Zanny wonder again why there had been no mention of the incident in the next day's paper, or the ones after that.

But the thought didn't occupy her for long. It never did, because as she read the article, her eyes kept being drawn away from the type to the little photograph beside it. It was a picture of the man suspected of both the robbery and the shooting death of the man named Taglia. Zanny stared at his face, at the wild black eyebrows, the large dark eyes, the strong straight nose, the thick dark hair. She held a thumb over the top of the man's head. No wonder her father had been so pleased about his thinning hair. It was amazing how much hair loss could alter a person's appearance. Zanny looked again at the name printed under the photograph: Michael Alexander. Special Agent Wiley hadn't lied to her. Her father hadn't been who she thought he was: good old Mitch Dugan. He had been a thief and murderer named Michael Alexander.

Chapter Seven

Zanny was drying the breakfast dishes for Mrs. Finster the next morning, wondering whether Special Agent Wiley had obtained a warrant yet, when the doorbell rang. Mrs. Finster rushed to answer it. Zanny continued to dry and stack dishes until she heard Lieutenant Jenkins's voice. Then she set her dishtowel aside. Maybe he had come to tell her something new about her father's death? She hurried into the front hall to find out.

Lieutenant Jenkins stood in the hall, talking to Mrs. Finster. He wasn't alone. Beside him was a tall red-headed man with a powerful build. The minute this man's pale blue eyes lit on Zanny, his face crinkled into a pleasant smile. He looked pleased to see her, which made no sense at all: the man was a complete stranger.

Mrs. Finster was smiling, too, as she wiped her wet hands on her apron.

"Wonderful news, Zanny," she announced.

"Lieutenant Jenkins has found your uncle."

Uncle? But that was impossible. Zanny didn't have an uncle. If she did, surely her father would have told her about him. But then, this wouldn't be the first thing her father had neglected to mention. She stared at the burly man, looking for something familiar, but of course she found nothing. She had never seen him before in her life.

Lieutenant Jenkins stepped forward and smiled at Zanny.

"How are you doing?" he asked. "Is everything okay?"

"I guess," Zanny said.

"That's good. That's very good. Because you know, Zanny, things are turning out to be a little more complicated than they first seemed. I'd like to talk to you about it." He glanced at Mrs. Finster. "Is there some place where we could speak to Zanny privately?"

Mrs. Finster nodded but looked hurt at being excluded. "Why don't you go into the living room. I'll make some fresh coffee."

"We wouldn't want to put you to any trouble," Lieutenant Jenkins said.

"A pot of coffee, how much trouble could it be?" She showed them in, then bustled back to the kitchen.

"Have a seat, Zanny," Lieutenant Jenkins said.

She chose one of Mrs. Finster's wing chairs. Lieutenant Jenkins took the other. The redheaded man sat down on the sofa and smiled at Zanny.

"I guess you don't remember me, Zanny," he said. "The last time I saw you, you were just a baby.

91

I'm your Uncle Everett. Everett Lloyd. I'm your mother's brother."

Zanny found that she wasn't really surprised. She realized that nothing could surprise her any more, not even the fact that her father had named her uncle as her guardian but had neglected to even tell her about him. Worse, had lied to her. Had told her that she had no relatives at all. Zanny turned to Lieutenant Jenkins.

"You said things are turning out to be complicated. What do you mean?"

Lieutenant Jenkins glanced at Everett Lloyd. Everett Lloyd nodded.

"It seems," Lieutenant Jenkins said slowly, "that your father wasn't exactly who everyone thought he was."

Zanny fought the urge to say, I know. She wanted to hear what the lieutenant had to say.

"I don't know how much he told you about your mother, Zanny."

"Only that she died in a car accident when I was little."

Lieutenant Jenkins and Everett Lloyd exchanged glances. Their solemnity indicated that they knew something she didn't. *Everybody* seemed to know things about her father that she didn't. It made Zanny angry.

"She *did* die in an accident, didn't she?" she demanded. "Look, if you know something different, I'd appreciate you telling me."

"Your mother did die in an accident," Everett Lloyd said. His voice was deep, but he spoke quietly. He kept his gaze steady, looking into her eyes as if he were looking into the window of a house, trying to see what was inside. Zanny had to struggle to keep from turning away. "Pretty soon after that, your father packed up and the two of you just disappeared. I've been trying to find you ever since."

Zanny studied the big man's pale blue eyes and saw nothing in them but sincerity.

"Well, now you found me. Or, should I say, the police found *you*."

"That's the funny part," Lieutenant Jenkins said. "I've been on the force for fifteen years and I've never seen a coincidence like it."

They were interrupted by Mrs. Finster, who came into the room carrying a tray laden with cups, cream, sugar, a coffee pot and a plate of shortbread cookies.

"Excuse me," she said as she bustled about, serving coffee, passing cream, sugar and cookies. "I don't mean to interrupt. I'll just be a minute."

The awkward silence that accompanied her activity was broken by Everett Lloyd, who praised Mrs. Finster's cookies. "I'd love the recipe," he said. "My wife is a good cook, but her shortbread is nothing like this."

Mrs. Finster flushed with pride. "I'll write it down for you," she offered, and left the room.

Zanny looked at Lieutenant Jenkins and said, "A coincidence like what?"

"The day after your father . . . " He hesitated. "The day after he died, I found a message on my desk. From Everett Lloyd. This was before William Sullivan informed me that an Everett Lloyd had been named in your father's will as your guardian. Even so, it took me a while to get back to him because of an ongoing investigation. And when I did, it turned out that he was calling for an identification on a newspaper photograph." Zanny's heart leapt into her throat. She wondered if he meant the same newspaper photograph she had found. "It turned out that it was a picture of you."

"Of *me?*" This was a new twist.

"It was a photograph of the demonstration in front of the Burger Shack a couple of weeks back. It ran in the newspaper here, and the Wilmington paper picked it up."

Zanny turned to Everett Lloyd. "You mean you've been searching for me since my mother died and all this time you were living as close as Wilmington?"

"I flew in from Chicago," Everett Lloyd said.

Chicago. Where the robbery had occurred. Zanny tried to maintain a blank expression, as if the name held no significance for her.

"It was only by chance that I even saw the newspaper photo. My wife ordered a birthday gift for me from an antique store in Wilmington. It arrived wrapped in a page of the Wilmington newspaper. As soon as I saw the picture, I started making phone calls."

Now Zanny was completely confused. She regarded the stranger with new suspicion. "I don't understand. You just said you hadn't seen me since I was a baby. How could you recognize me from a picture in the newspaper?"

Everett Lloyd's pale eyes grew moist. "How

could I *not* recognize you?" he said. "You look exactly like your mother when she was your age."

Zanny glanced over at Lieutenant Jenkins for confirmation. Was this true? Had this man really stumbled upon her whereabouts in such an odd way?

Lieutenant Jenkins shrugged. "This case is filled with coincidence," he said.

Coincidence didn't begin to cover it. Things were happening to her that she wouldn't believe if they happened to a character in a movie. She didn't know what to think about Everett Lloyd. His story was different from the one Wiley had told her. Everett Lloyd claimed that her father had left Chicago as a result of her mother's death. He hadn't said anything about the ten million dollars. What could that mean? That Everett Lloyd didn't know about the robbery? But he was from Chicago. Surely he had to know. Maybe he did, but was trying to keep it from Lieutenant Jenkins or Zanny. Which raised another set of questions, the biggest being, Why?

"How can you be sure he's my uncle?" she asked Lieutenant Jenkins. "Does he have any proof?" What kind of proof would a person need to make it conclusive that he was another person's uncle?

"That's where it gets even more complicated, Zanny," Lieutenant Jenkins replied. "Mr. Lloyd is a securities investigator in Chicago — quite a well-respected one, I understand. So I have no reason to doubt his claim. But you're a minor and the state can't just hand you into someone's care without going by the book. Mr. Lloyd has unfortunately been unable to produce a copy of your birth certificate, nor have we been able to find one among your father's papers. We're going to keep looking. Your parents weren't living in Chicago when you were born. In fact, Mr. Lloyd says he doesn't know where they were living at the time."

Zanny raised an eyebrow. "You didn't know where your own sister was living?"

"You father travelled a lot," Everett Lloyd said. "Your mother travelled with him. They didn't always tell us where they were."

"Why not?"

"To tell you the truth, my parents didn't approve of the marriage."

"You mean, they didn't approve of my father," Zanny said. It wasn't a question. It was a statement.

Everett Lloyd nodded. "We didn't even know she was pregnant until after you were born."

"Which means we don't know which hospital you were born in," Lieutenant Jenkins added, "or even what state. But we're looking. We're also working with Mr. Lloyd here and with the Chicago police to find anyone who knew your mother and father when they lived there. And of course we'll check for medical records . . . "

"Medical records?"

"For blood type. We won't be able to release you to Mr. Lloyd until we have all the paperwork done."

"Meaning what?"

"Meaning this could take a while. A few days at the most."

"And if you don't find anything?" Zanny asked. "If you can't prove he's my uncle, then what happens?"

"Why don't we cross that bridge if we come to it?" Lieutenant Jenkins said. "I'm sure everything will work out just fine."

Zanny wished she could feel as sure, but with everything that was happening, she didn't. She looked again at the man who claimed to be her uncle. If he really was, and if he lived in Chicago, then he must know more about her father. She decided to find out how much more.

"What about the DEA?" she asked.

Everett Lloyd's pale blue eyes widened with surprise. "The DEA?" he said. "What about them?"

Lieutenant Jenkins looked pained. "I'm afraid I'm not at liberty to say."

He didn't want to talk about it. Special Agent Wiley hadn't wanted to, either. Well, too bad for them. If it involved her father, Zanny had a right to talk about it.

"An agent from the DEA is here," she explained to Everett Lloyd. "He's been asking a lot of questions about my father. I think they might have something to do with how he died."

"Now, Zanny," Lieutenant Jenkins said, in a reasonable, calming tone of voice. "We don't know —"

"*I* know," Zanny said. "I know that whatever else my father was, he wasn't the kind of person who would kill himself."

"Now see here, Zanny," Lieutenant Jenkins began.

"The DEA wants to keep everything quiet. *You* want to keep everything quiet. No one wants to find out how my father really died. So *you* see here. If you don't start giving me some answers, I'm going to contact the newspapers and I'm going to tell them everything I know and I don't care what you or the DEA or anyone else thinks."

"That would not be a good idea," Everett Lloyd said quietly.

Lieutenant Jenkins looked at him. "How much do you know?"

"Probably as much as you do," Everett Lloyd said. "I know what they say Mike did."

Zanny looked at him sharply. "Mike?"

"Michael Alexander. That was his real name."

This much, at least, agreed with Wiley's story.

"I know about the ten million dollars that was stolen from the Pescis. I also know that Mike took off right after the money went missing."

Zanny's anger flared. "You think he did it? Is that what you're saying? You think my father is a thief?"

"I didn't say that."

"You didn't answer my question."

Everett Lloyd sighed. "Right now my opinion doesn't matter much, Zanny. Enough people believe your father did it to make it important that nobody finds out about any of this. If the word gets out who your father really was, it could attract some unsavoury types. And I don't think that would be very safe for you, Zanny. I think you should let the police — and the DEA — do their jobs. I think you should co-operate with them."

98

Zanny stared at the redheaded man. Who was he, anyway? Just a name in her father's will, someone her father had never mentioned to her, someone who claimed to be her uncle but whom she had never seen before in her life. She couldn't think of any reason to listen to him.

"You still didn't answer my questions," she said. "Do you think my father took the money?"

Everett Lloyd leaned back in his chair and sighed. He rubbed his eyes with one hand. "I know the facts, Zanny. I know your father was an undercover police officer who was under a lot of pressure. I know he left the police force. I know he got involved with some unsavoury people. And I know that ten million dollars disappeared at the same time you and your father did."

A cop? Her father had been a cop, and she had never known? Worse, her father had been a cop who had gone bad.

"But how?" Zanny asked. "Why would he do something like that?"

Everett Lloyd's broad shoulders heaved in an enormous shrug.

"I'd like to talk to you about all of this, Zanny. But first I'd like to get to know you a little better, and I'd like you to get to know me. In the meantime, I think we should keep the whole matter quiet. It's for your own good."

Lieutenant Jenkins drank the last of the coffee Mrs. Finster had poured for him. "I hope you'll listen to Mr. Lloyd," he said. "He makes a lot of sense. For your own safety, Zanny, you should keep out of this and let the professionals do their jobs."

He stood up and looked at Everett Lloyd. "I'll give you a ride back to your motel."

"Thanks, Lieutenant, but if Zanny doesn't mind, I'd like to take a few minutes to get acquainted."

Lieutenant Jenkins nodded. "I'll be in touch," he said. He went into the kitchen to say goodbye to Mrs. Finster.

Zanny stared icily at the redheaded man. "I have to go. I have to meet someone."

Everett Lloyd smiled benignly. "I won't keep you long. I guess this is all pretty strange for you. First, what happened to your father. And now me, popping into your life." He dug into his pants pocket and pulled out a wallet, which he flipped open. He hunted through, pulled out a small picture and handed it to her.

"I don't know whether you've seen this or not," he said. "It's your mother and father on their wedding day. I wasn't there. They were married in Las Vegas. But your mother sent this picture."

Zanny told herself she didn't want anything from this man. She told herself she didn't even want to be sitting in the same room with him. Just who did he think he was, waltzing into her life after all these years, pretending that he cared about her while telling her that her father was a thief? No wonder her father had seemed so bitter at times. His own brother-in-law believed he had stolen ten million dollars. His own brother-in-law didn't even try to defend him. She wanted to tell Everett Lloyd exactly what he could do with his stupid photograph. But she couldn't. She just couldn't pass up this chance.

She accepted the picture he offered her and stared hungrily at it, greedily drinking in every detail. The young man in the photo was unmistakably her father, although he was much thinner than she remembered him, with more hair — longer hair — than she had ever seen on him. He was dressed in a dove-grey tuxedo with a pink carnation boutonniere and he beamed at the slim dark woman beside him. It was the bride who really captured Zanny's attention. Suddenly she felt light-headed as she stared at the clear smiling face, the blue eyes, the thick chestnut hair. All her life she had wondered where she got her looks. She didn't resemble her father at all, she had inherited none of his features. Most of her friends looked like one their parents; Zanny looked like no one. Until now. It was like looking into a mirror.

"It's uncanny," Everett Lloyd said. "When I saw that newspaper picture, I couldn't believe my eyes. I could have sworn I was looking at a picture of Jenny fifteen or twenty years ago."

"Jenny," Zanny echoed. One of the few things she knew about her mother was her name. In the past two days, however, she had found herself wondering if that had been real, or if it was just another thing her father had made up, just another lie.

"Jennifer Anne Lloyd," Everett Lloyd said. "You look just like her." He pulled another picture from his wallet and handed it to her. "This is Jenny and me when we were kids. I was five years older than she was." The photo showed a younger, less bulky Everett Lloyd with his arm around the same slim young woman. "She was beautiful, wasn't she?

And talented. She was a dancer, you know."

Zanny looked at him in surprise. She hadn't known. She knew almost nothing about her mother except that she had died, that it was a long time ago, and that her father didn't like to talk about it.

"She gave up dancing when she married your father," Everett Lloyd said. His eyes misted over. "She gave up a lot of things."

Zanny looked sharply at him. What was that supposed to mean? Was this man criticizing her father?

Everett Lloyd's face reddened. "I'm sorry, I didn't mean . . . " He gazed at the photos and started to slip them back into his wallet. Then he stopped. He handed one to Zanny, the one of her parents on their wedding day. "Maybe you'd like to keep this one."

Zanny accepted it silently. She didn't know what to make of this man. She looked into his pale blue eyes.

"What happens now?"

Everett Lloyd tucked his wallet back into his pocket. "I guess I wait," he answered. "I'm staying at the motel up on the interstate. We'll wait until all the paperwork is taken care of. Then we'll have to get busy."

"Get busy? What do you mean?"

"We'll have to get you packed up and ready to go. I'm sure you'll like Chicago, Zanny. It's a great city. And, of course, we'll have to deal with all the loose ends here, the house, all of your father's belongings. We'll have to decide what can be kept and what will have to be disposed of." He stood up.

"I have a few things I have to take care of today, but I'd like it very much if we could have dinner together. I could pick you up here around six o'clock."

Zanny nodded slowly. She had always known she couldn't stay with Mrs. Finster indefinitely, but she hadn't thought she would have to move as far away as Chicago. It seemed silly after all the moves she had made in her life that one more should matter, but it did. Suddenly she couldn't imagine leaving the little red brick house next door. She'd lived in it for only a year, but it was her home.

"Zanny?"

She looked at her uncle.

"Are you okay?"

She nodded.

"Good." He smiled at her. "I think I'll just have a few words with Mrs. Finster before I leave."

Zanny watched as he went into the kitchen.

Chapter Eight

After Everett Lloyd left, Zanny sat alone in Mrs. Finster's living room, feeling numb. At first, Special Agent Wiley had been the only person who said that her father was a thief. Not any more. It was turning into a majority decision against her father. Lieutenant Jenkins said he was a thief. The old newspaper clipping she had found had said he was a thief. His own brother-in-law — her uncle — said he was a thief.

She didn't believe them — at least, she didn't *want* to believe them. Sure, her dad was a loner. Sure, he had moved them around a lot over the years. But she knew him to be an honest man who had raised her to be honest. She knew him as a man who was respected by his co-workers. Besides, if he had stolen all that money, wouldn't they have lived better? Wiley and the others had to be wrong. He had to be innocent. Maybe he'd been framed. But how could Zanny prove that everybody was wrong about her father?

She could think of only one way. She had to prove that there was no ten million dollars, that there never had been. She had to search her house from top to bottom, inside and out, and prove that the money didn't exist.

She was halfway up the driveway to her house, keys clasped in her hand, when someone called her name. She turned, saw Nick down by the road and raised a hand to him. She had intended to search the house, even if it took all day. But she couldn't tell Nick that. Nor did she want to tell him to go away, at least not in any way that he might misinterpret. She didn't want him think that she wasn't interested in seeing him again. She said the first thing that came into her head.

"What are you doing here?"

He reacted to the question with mild sarcasm. "I'm fine, thanks," he said. "How are you?"

Zanny felt her cheeks redden. "I'm sorry. I didn't mean that the way it sounded."

"It's just that you're not exactly thrilled to see me, right?"

"No, really, it's not that."

"But? I know there's a 'but' coming. What's the matter, Zanny?"

"Nothing." Her voice rose uncertainly at the end of the word, betraying her.

Nick's brown eyes filled with concern. "Something's bothering you, Zanny, and I don't just mean what happened to your father. Something *else* is wrong. It was wrong last night in the library and it's wrong now. It has to do with that guy from the DEA, doesn't it? He told you something, and whatever he told you is eating you alive. I cut class to come over and make sure you're okay." He peered into her eyes for a moment. When she didn't answer, he sighed and shrugged.

"Okay," he said, "no problem. I get the picture. Whatever it is, you don't want to tell me about it. I guess I can handle that." But he didn't do a very good job of keeping the hurt from his voice. "Look, if you want me to go, just say the word, and I'll go. Maybe I can even get to school in time for algebra class."

"It's not that I *want* you to go," she said. "I just . . ." Just what? Just want to be alone so that I can ransack my own house. You see, I'm half afraid there's ten million dollars in there somewhere and I have to tear the place apart to prove that there isn't. Or — and this was the part that really scared her, the part that made her knees turn to overcooked spaghetti — until I find it. If she said that, he'd think she was crazy for sure.

Nick reached out and touched her shoulder. "I'm sorry," he said. "You've been through a lot. You don't need me to make you feel any worse than you already do. I'll call you later. Maybe you'll feel like going out and doing something, you know, to get your mind off things." Then, so swiftly, so gently that he took her breath away with the surprise and the delight of it, his soft warm lips met hers. She had been kissed before, once, by a boy she didn't even particularly like; she had only let him do it because he had been the first boy who had ever asked her to a dance. That kiss had felt nothing like this. She had never felt lightning surge through her the way it did now, energizing her and draining her all at once.

"I'll call you later," he said, each word a sweet whisper in her ear. His lips touched hers again and lingered this time. One of his hands brushed softly against her cheek, the other held her chin lightly. Her knees weakened. She wished he would go on kissing her forever. Slowly he pulled away.

"Nick?"

She felt lost in his eyes. He was so under-standing, so sweet. And he cared about her. He was ready to give her as much time and space as she needed. Being with him was like being with Lily, comfortable and connected. She felt she was with someone who really knew her.

"Nick, if I tell you something, do you promise you won't tell anyone?"

He frowned. "Something *is* wrong, isn't it, Zanny? This has something to do with that DEA guy, doesn't it? It has something to do with what we were looking for in the library last night."

She nodded and climbed the steps to the house to unlock the door, then looked back at Nick, who was still standing in the driveway. He climbed the stairs and followed her into the house.

"What's going on, Zanny?"

"I found out why the DEA is interested in my father."

Nick said nothing, but from his sombre expression she knew he'd guessed it wasn't good news.

"They say he was a cop who couldn't handle temptation." At least, that's what Everett Lloyd had implied. "They say that he stole ten million dollars in drug money." There, she'd uttered the ridiculous accusation aloud — and no one was laughing. Nick gazed at her solemnly.

"Do you believe that, Zanny?"

"I don't know what to believe. You don't know what it's like, Nick. You think you know someone. He was my father. We lived together for sixteen years, and I really thought I knew him. Now everyone is telling me he wasn't who he said he was. Mitch Dugan wasn't even his name. His real name was Michael Alexander."

Nick gazed at her blankly.

"And then I found this . . . " She pulled the folded photocopy from her jeans pocket and handed it to him. As he unfolded it, she said, "It was even in the newspaper. Michael Alexander stole ten million dollars from a major organized crime family and took off. Look at that picture. You never met my father. Well, meet him now. Nick Mulaney, meet Mitch Dugan, alias Michael Alexander. Meet Melissa Alexander, a.k.a. Zanny Dugan."

"A.k.a.?"

"Also known as."

Nick smoothed out the sheet of paper and read the story slowly. He looked back up at Zanny.

"This is your father?"

Zanny nodded. "I found that in the library last night. I didn't want to tell you. I was too . . . ashamed."

"Ashamed? Of what? Zanny, whatever your father did or didn't do, it was him, it wasn't you. You said it yourself, you didn't even know anything about it. Why should you be ashamed?"

She looked down at the tile on the foyer floor. It was a good question, one she didn't know how to answer.

"I just . . . I don't know. Nick, everyone is saying that my father was a criminal. They say he stole ten million dollars. *Ten million*."

Nick nodded slowly. "But if he did, there's nothing you can do about it."

If. It was a little word that meant a lot.

"The man from the DEA is here to try to find the ten million dollars."

"Find it?" Nick shook his head. "That guy must be dreaming in Technicolor. No one who stole ten million dollars . . . " His voice trailed off. "I'm sorry."

"It's okay," Zanny said. "Go ahead. You were saying?"

"No one who goes to all the trouble of stealing ten million dollars is going to leave it just lying around. He's going to spend it. He's going to blow the whole wad."

"That's exactly the point. You'd think if we had lots of money, we'd be living in a big house. But we aren't. We never have. Most of the places we've lived in have been smaller than this."

"What are you getting at, Zanny?"

"We've always lived in small, cheap places. We've always eaten at cheap fast-food restaurants, the kind my father could afford on whatever wage he was earning doing mostly unskilled work. We never had any money, Nick. We never even took a decent vacation, ever. I think that's because my dad never took the money. But suppose he did. If my dad took that money like everyone says he did, he sure didn't spend it. Not on me, anyway. Not on himself. Which means that if he took it, it's still around somewhere. I'm going to search the house, Nick. Either I'm going to find that money, or I'm going to prove that he never took it. It may not be much, but it's better than sitting around doing nothing."

She was relieved to see that Nick wasn't laughing at her. In fact, he nodded solemnly.

"Do you want some help?" he asked.

* * *

"It seems to me that the best way to look for something," Nick said, "is to start at the bottom and work your way to the top. Or vice versa."

This made sense. Zanny didn't want to overlook anything. After a few moments of deliberation, they decided to start at the bottom. They trudged down to the unfinished basement.

Zanny looked at the large, open, cement-floored room, at the washing machine and dryer in one corner, at the open shelves of boots and ice-skates and cross-country ski boots, at the small stack of cardboard cartons.

"This shouldn't take too long," she said.

Nick surveyed the room more slowly. "That depends."

"On what?"

"On what exactly we're searching for. What do you think ten million dollars looks like?"

She hadn't given the matter much thought.

"Do you mean, what denominations?"

Nick shrugged. "Maybe. But maybe it's not in

cash at all. Ten million dollars in cash — even in big bills like fifties and hundreds — is a lot of cash, a lot of bills. It would take up space, maybe a large suitcase or a box or trunk or something like that. If someone really wanted to hide that amount of cash, maybe they'd hide it in a false wall or a secret compartment of some kind. Or maybe it isn't cash. Maybe it's gold or diamonds, or bonds or something that can be easily converted into cash. Or maybe the actual ten million isn't here at all. He got it out of the country somehow and it's in a Swiss bank account or in a bank in the Cayman Islands. It could be we're looking for some kind of passbook."

Zanny stared at him in silence for a few moments. She hadn't considered any of those possibilities. What had at first seemed like a simple enough job — search a small house for a large amount of money — was turning out to be an impossible mission.

"So what does that mean?" Zanny said. "What exactly *are* we looking for?"

"I guess that's the trick," Nick answered. "Whatever it is, we'll have to look carefully. And I guess it wouldn't hurt to check the walls for hollow compartments and false doors."

"It sounds like something out of a movie." In fact, the whole thing sounded like something out of a movie. Or out of a nightmare.

They started together in one corner of the basement, checking the toes of ice-skates and ski boots for stashes of diamonds, the linings of old winter garments for bonds sewn into them, the walls behind the shelves for a hidden compartment.

"Nothing," Zanny concluded after they had combed the place. "Shall we?"

Nick nodded and followed her up to the main floor of the house.

"I guess there's not much point in going through the kitchen cupboards," she said. "I do most of the cooking. If there was anything hidden in here, I would have found it a long time ago."

"Maybe," Nick said. "Maybe not. The bottom of the flour canister could be a good place to hide something. Maybe it has a false bottom. Or there might be some old container in the freezer that you never noticed."

Zanny regarded him with playful suspicion. "Where do you get all these ideas?"

He grinned sheepishly. "I'm addicted to mystery novels," he said. "I can't help it."

"Well, it sure is coming in handy. I guess we'd better get busy, huh?"

She had never thought of her kitchen as large. In fact, when she and her father were both in it, working together to prepare the evening meal, it had sometimes seemed impossibly small. Now she saw that it all depended on what you were doing there. When she was cooking, desperate for counter space, the kitchen seemed minuscule. Now that she was searching it for loot, it seemed immense, containing a thousand objects and items to be peered into, emptied, and refilled. And after scrupulously investigating every inch of it, she was rewarded with exactly nothing.

While she worked in the kitchen, Nick made his way through the living room and dining room. She heard him tapping walls and overturning furniture. As Zanny put the last of the canisters back into the cupboard, her stomach growled again.

"Nick? Nick, are you hungry?"

Nick appeared, smiling, in the kitchen doorway.

"Starving," he said.

Zanny peered into the refrigerator. There wasn't much, and what there was had been there for almost a week. She sniffed the milk and made a face: it had gone sour. The lettuce in the crisper was wilted and black at the edges. The little bit of cheese that remained was spotted with mould. She turned to the cupboards instead. "There's soup," she announced. "And crackers."

"Sounds good to me," Nick said.

While Zanny heated the soup, Nick set out bowls and spoons and the box of crackers. She ladled the soup out, then joined him at the table.

"You must think this is pretty crazy," she commented as she watched him spoon up soup.

"Not at all. I've spent some of the best times of my life searching people's houses for millions of dollars."

"You're kidding."

"Yes and no. Yes, in that I've never done this before. And no, in that this has been a great day, Zanny. But then, I think any day would be great so long as I got to spend it with you."

Zanny ducked her head to hide her blush. She ate a little soup.

"I've been thinking," she said slowly. "If we don't find anything here, that doesn't mean he didn't do it, does it?"

"I hate to say it, but no. I mean, he could have hidden the money somewhere else. He could have left something with a friend, you know, like a key to a safety deposit box."

"He didn't have many friends. My father liked to keep to himself."

"Maybe he had a lawyer. Maybe he left something with his lawyer. A lot of people do that. A lot of lawyers hold things for their clients."

Zanny frowned. She hadn't considered that. "But Mr. Sullivan didn't mention anything about that."

"Mr. Sullivan?"

"William Sullivan, my father's lawyer. He drew up Dad's will." She thought for a moment. "He had a file folder with my father's name on it. I suppose it's possible he could have something in there that might help us. But if he did, wouldn't he have told me?" Zanny's father had left everything he owned to her: the will had been quite explicit. "I think we should keep looking here," she said. "Then, if we don't find anything, I'll talk to Mr. Sullivan."

"Sounds like a plan to me." Nick finished his soup and carried his bowl to the sink. "So," he asked, "are we ready to graduate to the second floor?"

She nodded, and together they climbed the stairs. They were at they top before Zanny realized she had a problem. A big problem. Apart from the bathroom, there were only two rooms on the second floor: hers and her father's. At first she thought that her room didn't need to be searched. After all, if something was hidden in it, she would know, wouldn't she? Maybe not. She could almost see the logic to it: who would suspect? Her room would be the last place she'd ever think to look, and therefore one of the most obvious hiding places.

She was starting to sound like Nick, suspecting everything, taking nothing for granted. She certainly didn't want Nick searching her room. Who knew what she might have left lying around. It could be really embarrassing.

But she couldn't let him search her father's room, either, because she didn't know what was in there. Her father might have hidden more than just the missing ten million dollars. He might have hidden something from the past — *her* past — a few clues, a few bits and pieces. She didn't want Nick to find those. She wanted to do it herself.

She stopped at the top of the stairs.

Nick stopped beside her and looked at the two bedrooms. Then he looked over and studied her for a moment.

"Does this place have an attic?" he asked.

"An attic?"

"Sure. Attics are great hiding places. If there's an attic, I can search up there. You can do the bedrooms."

She looked gratefully at him and nodded.

"The entrance is there." She pointed to a panel in the ceiling of the upstairs hall. "There's a step-ladder in the basement."

"I'll get it."

As he started down the stairs, Zanny looked at the two bedrooms again. She would have to do both of them. There was no avoiding the inevitable. But

115

her father wasn't around to tell her to be a good girl, to eat her spinach first and save her ice cream as a reward for a job well done. She could at least postpone the inevitable. She went to her own room first and tapped the walls and the floor in the closet. She worked methodically, pulling out her furniture, looking behind her desk and her dresser for false backs where something could be hidden, checking under her bed for loose floorboards. She found nothing.

And then there was no more putting it off. In all the time that she had been dreading it, it hadn't gone away. It was still there, waiting for her.

Zanny walked down the hall and crossed the threshold into her father's bedroom. Over the years, she had been in more than a dozen rooms where her father had slept, but she had not often been in his one. By the time they had moved into this house, she and her father had grown apart. She kept enough distance from him to let him know exactly how she felt about his unreasonable curfews, and how eagerly she looked forward to the day when she could go her own way. In this house, her room had been her refuge; her father's room had often been enemy territory.

The first thing she noticed was that it held a faint smell of his spicy aftershave. She must have bought him gallons of the stuff over the years, for Christmas, for his birthday, for Father's Day. He was so hard to shop for that almost every year she got him aftershave or talc or soap-on-a-rope to mark one of those occasions. He always looked surprised; he always professed to be pleased. "This is what *my* dad used to wear," he said. She wondered now if that was true, or just something he had made up, like his name.

Zanny noticed how excruciatingly neat the room was. Her own was much more casually arranged; she loved to have her possessions cluttered around her. He seemed to have so few.

The covers on his bed had been pulled up and tucked in tightly. Nothing but a telephone sat on his bedside table. The top of his chest of drawers was spotless. A lone book lay atop the chest at the foot of his bed.

Zanny stepped cautiously around the bed. Her fingers trembled as she reached for the handle of the drawer in the bedside table. This was where Lieutenant Jenkins had found the gun and the bullets that had killed her father. She pulled it open. It was empty except for the local telephone directory.

Next she went to the chest of drawers and pulled open the top drawer, where he kept his brush and his comb, a few ties laid out in a row and two tie-tacks, one onyx, one silver. She felt around the edges of the drawer the way she had seen Nick do in the kitchen, tapping them, listening for a false bottom or side.

Nothing.

She opened the next drawer and immediately felt funny about plunging her hand inside. It was her father's underwear drawer. (Ah, but it's obvious, she heard Nick say, the perfect hiding place.) Gingerly, she pulled out the neatly folded underwear, tapped and listened, then replaced it. She worked her way through all the drawers, felt all the clothing for the stiffness of bond paper.

Nothing.

She closed the last drawer and turned to the chest at the foot of the bed. She removed the book and set it onto the bed. Then she pulled up the lid and breathed in the sweet aroma of cedar. The trunk was filled with neatly folded sweaters and jackets.

She lifted the sweaters out one by one until she came to something that wasn't a sweater. She pulled a small, flat box from the trunk and held her breath as she opened it. Whatever was inside had been wrapped in layers of tissue paper, which she now carefully peeled aside. Her eyes widened in surprise as she plucked from the box a tiny white gown. Her own tiny white gown, she realized, probably the one she had worn on the day of her christening. All this time she had never known it existed. She refolded it gently into its cocoon of tissue paper and set the box aside.

Once more she delved into the trunk and once more she brought forth something that was not a sweater. Her hands trembled as she lifted the heavy object: here was something else she'd never known existed. A photograph album. All these years he had told her there were no pictures, they had all been burned, and all these years he had kept a photograph album hidden at the bottom of his trunk. She sat cross-legged on the floor with the album on her lap. Her fingers shook as she opened the cover.

Zanny sighed with disappointment. The book was filled with photos, but none of them were of her or her mother. In fact, the only face she recognized was that of her father. All of the photos had been taken in bedrooms — well, the rooms had been decorated to look like bedrooms, with bright wallpaper, nice furniture and pretty pictures on the walls. But the bed in each of them was a hospital bed, and the person, the child, in each one looked gaunt and fevered. The photographs had all been taken at the hospital, Zanny realized. Under each photo, penned in strong black print, was a name and a date. Preceding each date was the letter *d*. Tucked into many of the pages, between the plastic-coated pages, were cards and notes, all to her father, all thanking him. Thanking a hospital orderly. Zanny recalled the words of the hospital librarian and the nurse on the children's ward. "Your father was so good to them," they had said. "He knew how to make them happy." She struggled with the image, tried to picture her father cheering a small, sick child. She leafed through the album, and read the notes. Some were written in the awkward block print or wobbly hand of a child. Some were from people who bore the same last name as the children, and who mentioned the children in their messages. Mothers and fathers, Zanny thought, of children who had died.

As she worked her way through the album, reading the cards and notes, tears gathered in her eyes. She had hardly ever spoken to her father about his work. She hadn't even been interested. After all, he was just an orderly.

She closed the album. As she stood up to return it to the chest, something slipped out from between the pages and fell to the floor. An envelope. Probably another grateful note. She picked it up, then read the words on the outside: *To be opened in the event of my death.* She opened her mouth to call for Nick, to tell him she had found something, maybe the something they were looking for. But the slam of the door downstairs, followed by a shout, stopped her. She stuffed the envelope into her jeans pocket, buried the album again under the heap of sweaters in the chest and closed the lid.

"Who's there?" she called.

Immediately she heard footsteps coming toward her from two directions. From above, the clatter of Nick's feet coming down the ladder, and from below, several pairs of feet mounting the stairs. Nick, Wiley and two uniformed police officers appeared in the upstairs hallway together.

"What are you doing here?" Zanny said to Wiley. "Who gave you permission to come into my house?"

Wiley looked almost apologetic as he delved into his jacket pocket and produced a document. "The court gave me permission. I'm sorry, Zanny, but I told you, I have a job to do, and I intend to do it. These two officers," he nodded over his shoulder at the two policemen, "are here to help me."

Zanny looked at Nick, who shrugged. She knew he was right. They could do nothing, not when Wiley had two policemen with him.

"Come on, Zanny," Nick said. "Let's get out of here."

Zanny brushed by Wiley and followed Nick down the stairs and out of the house. She was bursting to tell him what she had discovered. But as they went out the front door and started down the walk, she suddenly found herself face to face with Everett Lloyd.

"Mrs. Finster told me you were here," he said with a smile. He looked at the jeans and T-shirt she was wearing, then glanced at his watch. "I guess I'm a little early."

Zanny glanced at her own watch. It was five minutes after six. He wasn't early. She was late.

"I'll go get changed," she said quickly. "Call me tomorrow, okay, Nick?"

Nick nodded and kissed her lightly on the cheek. Zanny walked with her uncle to Mrs. Finster's house, her cheeks ablaze, the envelope she had found burning a hole in her jeans pocket.

"Where would you like to go for dinner?" Everett Lloyd asked.

"There isn't much choice," she informed him. "There's the Burger Shack. There's Alice's, where the bus stops, and the truckers like to go. And there's Diamond Jim's Place for Steak out on the interstate."

Chapter Nine

Zanny sat opposite her uncle in a booth at the back of Diamond Jim's Place for Steak.

"Do you see anything you like?" he asked. He was smiling. He always seemed to be smiling.

She had been staring at the menu for more than five minutes, but she hadn't really been reading it. She had been thinking about the envelope she had left in her suitcase under Mrs. Finster's dentist son's bed. She shouldn't have left it there. She should have tucked it into her purse and brought it with her. That way there would be absolutely no chance anyone would find it and read it before she had the chance to look at it. Besides, if she had brought it with her, she could have excused herself and gone into the ladies' room to open it. By now she could have known exactly what was in it.

"Zanny?" Everett Lloyd prodded gently. "Have you decided what you'd like to eat?" He nodded to a hovering waiter.

Flustered, she shook her head.

"Do you like steak or would you prefer something else?" he asked. "Grilled chicken, maybe? Or veal. Do you like veal?"

Zanny glanced at the menu. "I guess I'll have the chicken."

He gave the waiter her order and chose a steak for himself. When the waiter collected their menus, Zanny found herself with nothing to hide behind. She had to look at her uncle. This time he was the one to look away. He played with the stem of his water goblet for a few moments. When he looked at her again, he was no longer smiling.

"I spoke with the police again this afternoon, and with Children's Aid," he said. Zanny's stomach filled with butterflies, all beating their wings. She wasn't sure she wanted to hear this. "They followed up with some friends of the family in Chicago — people who knew both me and your mother. It seems they're satisfied that I am your uncle — and that you're my niece."

The waiter slid a green salad in front of Zanny and another in front of Everett Lloyd. Zanny picked up her fork and poked at the lettuce.

"Because of that, and because of the provisions in your father's will, I'm responsible for you now. We need to talk about this, Zanny. We have to decide what you're going to do."

The implications sank in slowly. The man sitting across the table from her now had complete control over her. Maybe the authorities were satisfied that he was her uncle, but to her, he was a complete stranger. Yet he was responsible for her. The details of her life were now up to him. It was up to him to set her curfew, to decide who she could go out with and when, to decide where she would live.

Zanny lost interest in her salad. It was up to him where she would live. And since he lived in Chicago, that meant that she would have to move there, too. She would have to leave Birks Falls and the little brick house at the top of the hill. She would have to leave the tall grass and the morning mists and the peaceful warbling of the sparrows and the wrens. And she would have to leave Nick.

Another leaving. She didn't think she could stand it. Chicago was so far away. Not as far as Germany and Lily, but far enough to make it difficult, if not impossible, for Nick to visit her or for her to visit him. And what if it turned out that she didn't like Chicago, or her uncle, or her aunt? It wasn't fair. This wasn't at all what she wanted. Without anyone even consulting her, a decision had been made about her entire future, and it wasn't the one she would have made for herself.

She took the linen napkin from her lap, placed it on the table, and started to get up.

"Zanny, please don't go." Everett Lloyd touched her hand. "I want to talk to you. I don't want to turn your life upside down. That's not what I'm here for. I'd like to know what *you* want."

"I can tell you what I *don't* want," she said. "I don't want to move to Chicago."

"Then let's talk about it. Maybe we can work something out."

She eyed him with suspicion. "You mean, work something out so that I don't have to go?"

"Not if you're dead set against it."

"But you said you're responsible for me . . . "

"Mrs. Finster has offered to let you stay with her."

"She has?"

Everett Lloyd nodded.

Zanny replaced the napkin on her lap and regarded him with new interest.

"How did that subject happen to come up?" she asked. "Did she raise it or did you?"

"She did. She thought you might need a little more time to say goodbye to your father."

Zanny was surprised. She liked Mrs. Finster and was grateful to her, but she had never guessed that she would be so understanding.

"I told her I thought it was a good idea," he said. "We — my wife Margaret and I — would love you to come and live with us in Chicago, Zanny. We think it would be good for you to be with your family. But we don't want to make you come until you're ready. You could live with Mrs. Finster at least until the end of the school year. Maybe you can find a summer job here. And maybe you could visit for a few days. Who knows? You might even decide that you like Chicago. At the very least, you'll get to meet your aunt and your cousins."

Cousins? This was news. "You have children?"

"A boy and a girl. Trish is six. Rob is eight."

Zanny tried to imagine him with kids calling him Daddy. He fished in his pocket and brought out a wallet. Out came more photographs. She admired the two children and how much they looked like their father. She remembered the picture of her mother that he had given her, and how much *she* looked like her mother.

"What was my mother like?" Zanny asked.

Her uncle paused a moment, then a smile spread slowly across this face. "As a kid sister, she could be a real pain in the neck. She trailed around after me all the time. Mom used to send her on dates with me, to make sure I acted like a gentleman." He grinned. "I used to give her money to go and buy candy. Considering how much of the stuff she consumed, it's amazing she stayed as skinny as she did." He sighed. "I remember the day she was born, you know. I went to see my mother in the hospital, and they let me hold her. She was four hours old."

A bittersweet smile played across his face as he stared into space. Then his gaze returned to Zanny. "Your mother was a wonderful dancer. She started ballet lessons at six. It was as if she was born to it. Then she discovered modern dance. I used to turn off the television every time I came across one of those old dancing movies — I thought they were ridiculous. I thought dancing was stupid until the first time I saw your mother on stage. She was fourteen, and she was breathtaking. She danced until just before she had her first . . . well, until she became a mother. You look just like her, Zanny."

"Do you . . . " She hesitated. This was so strange. She was sitting across from a man who she hadn't even known existed yesterday, a man who knew so much about the mother she couldn't remember at all. "Do you have any more pictures of her?"

He gave her a gentle smile. There was something comforting about it, something warm. She wondered if her mother had smiled like that. He dipped into his jacket pocket and pulled out a thick envelope, which he handed to her.

"I thought you might want to know more. I went through the photo albums before I left Chicago."

Zanny opened the envelope and looked inside. It contained a couple of dozen photographs. She stared at them like a beggar standing before a sumptuous feast. Her hand shook as she pulled them from the envelope.

"That's your mother when she was a little girl," Zanny's uncle said. "She was three in that picture. She talked non-stop when she was three, I remember, and every other word was *why*? Why is the sky blue? Why do giraffes have long necks? Why do lions have long hair, and why only male lions, why not females? Men lions and lady lions, she called them. And that next one . . . "

Zanny looked at the next picture — a little girl missing a tooth, smiling at the camera.

" . . . that was taken on her fifth birthday. She must have got a dozen Barbie dolls that year. That was all she wanted, Barbie dolls."

Zanny's mother grew up before her eyes as Zanny turned from picture to picture to picture. Their meals arrived. Zanny ate, but tasted nothing. She was entranced by the photographs and by the stories her uncle was recounting. They were all she heard, all she cared about.

Then, with her mother's marriage to her father, the photos suddenly stopped.

"What happened?" Zanny asked.

Pain flickered in her uncle's eyes. "You mean, the . . . accident?"

Zanny nodded. No one had ever told her — not the whole story. Her father would lapse into long dark silences whenever she asked, so she had stopped. The same pall now fell over her uncle.

"It was a car accident," he said.

"What kind of car accident?" A hundred possibilities suggested themselves to Zanny, as well as countless reasons why her father never wanted to discuss it. "Was my father in the car when it happened? Was it his fault?"

Her uncle leaned back in his chair and reached for his wine glass. "What did your father tell you?"

"Nothing. He never told me anything. I want to know. Did he . . . was he in any way responsible for my mother's death?"

Zanny's uncle sat perfectly still for a moment, then shook his head. "I don't think so, Zanny. To the best of my knowledge, he wasn't."

The waiter arrived with the bill. Her uncle smiled, this time a little too easily, with little of the previous warmth.

"Well," he said, "it's getting late. I'd better get you back to Mrs. Finster's. You can think about what I suggested. We can talk tomorrow." He stopped at the front door, chatted a few moments with Mrs. Finster and then left.

Zanny went upstairs. She put the envelope of photos on the dresser, sat down on the bed, leaned over and slid out her suitcase. She opened it and dug into one of its pockets to retrieve the envelope she had hidden there. She held it in her hand for a moment, staring at the handwriting she knew so well. She wondered what her father had been thinking when he wrote those words, whether he had written them expecting them to be read so soon.

She hooked her little finger under the envelope flap and tore along the fold. Two sheets of paper were inside. She pulled them out and unfolded them. The first sheet held her father's small, looped handwriting. Slowly, she read the note.

Dear Zanny,

I have started to write this a hundred times and it never comes out right. It's so difficult to be writing this, knowing that if you ever read it, it will be because I am dead. No one likes to think about that.

I can't tell you everything. It's too long, too complicated, and I'm not sure it makes sense even to me. But I can tell you I did what I felt I had to do at the time. If I had it to do over again, I'm not sure I would do it the same way, but there's no point in wishing to undo the past. Maybe the best I can do is apologize for it.

I know that what I did made your life harder than it needed to be, and I'm sorry. I never meant to hurt you. I hope you can believe that, and that when you remember me, you remember the good things. Be strong, Teddy Bear. I love you.

Dad.

Zanny stared at the paper through tear-blurred eyes, wishing she had never found it. *I did what I felt I had to do at the time.* She didn't want to believe it, but it was true. He was admitting that he had done what everyone accused him of. He'd had regrets, but he was admitting it. *I know that my actions have made your life harder . . .* He had stolen ten million dollars, and because of that, her whole life had been turned upside-down. All these years, he had been lying to his own daughter. He'd raised her to believe things that were never true. All these years, she hadn't even known her own real name. She crumpled the sheet of paper and threw it across the room. Damn him.

. . . remember the good things.

Be strong, Teddy Bear.

He must have written the note a long time ago. Zanny couldn't remember the last time her father had called her Teddy Bear, but it had been years. She remembered how she had loved the name. It had always made her feel special, and close to him.

She got up off the bed and slowly walked across the room to retrieve the ball of crumpled paper. Gently, she smoothed it out and refolded it, then set it carefully onto the bedside table.

I love you. Dad.

I love you, too, Daddy. I miss you. I miss you so much.

She wiped a tear away as she unfolded the second piece of paper that had been in the envelope. Written on it in large, black, block letters was a series of letters and numbers: WS105.5F2P2291909. Letters and numbers, with no pattern she could discern. Gibberish. They could mean anything. Or nothing.

No, not nothing. A man didn't write down a

meaningless jumble of letters and numbers, then seal it in an envelope marked *To be opened in the event of my death.* Especially not a man who had stolen ten million dollars. The letters and numbers had to mean something. They were the clue she had been looking for. If she could decipher them, she would locate the missing money. But *how* to decipher their meaning — that was the trick.

WS105.5. What could that be? Letters standing for numbers and numbers standing for letters? Maybe. *W* was the twenty-third letter of the alphabet, *S* the nineteenth. The number 105 would be *JE*. 2319JE? Zanny stared in frustration at the piece of paper. It was a code, but what code? And where was the key? *What* was the key?

She stared and stared at the piece of paper, but nothing came. After a while, she folded it back into its envelope and tucked it into her suitcase. It had to mean something. There had to be some way to decode it. But when she closed her eyes, it wasn't the mystery code that danced before them. It was her father's face, mouthing three simple words, words she wished he had said aloud more often. Her pillow was damp by the time she fell asleep.

* * *

She slept so poorly that when Mrs. Finster roused her, it felt like the middle of the night. In fact, the clock on her bedside table read a quarter past seven. Still, Zanny was groggily surprised. Mrs. Finster had been letting her sleep for as long as she wanted. But now she bustled around Zanny's room, opening the blinds and tossing Zanny her robe.

"The lieutenant is waiting downstairs," she said.

"You'd better hurry."

Zanny blinked as she sat up in bed. "The lieutenant?"

"Lieutenant Jenkins. He wants to talk to you. There's been a murder."

Chapter Ten

Lieutenant Jenkins was sitting in Mrs. Finster's living room drinking coffee from a china cup whose handle was too small for his hand. He looked like a giant holding a child's teacup. He put the cup down and got to his feet when Zanny came into the room.

"I'm sorry to get you out of bed," he said. "I waited as long as I could before coming over."

There were deep circles under his eyes. He looked as if he had been up all night.

"Mrs. Finster said that Mr. Sullivan is dead."

Lieutenant Jenkins nodded. "I'm afraid that's right."

"She said he was murdered. Is that true, too?"

The lieutenant nodded again. "He was killed last night. Apparently he was struck on the head with a heavy object. His office was ransacked."

"I hardly knew him," Zanny said. "I only met him once. Why do you want to talk to me about it?"

"Because of something we found in his waste-paper basket. Sit down, Zanny."

She sat. "What did you find?"

"A file. Most of it was burned — in fact, almost all of it. Just about all that was left was the label. It was your father's file, Zanny."

Her father's file. The thick file documenting all the business Mr. Sullivan had taken care of for her father. The *confidential* file.

"We have no idea who burned it, Sullivan or his killer, and we have no idea whether it was burned before Sullivan was murdered or after. But it appears to be the only file in the office that was destroyed."

As Zanny digested the news, Lieutenant Jenkins gulped down the remainder of his coffee. Then he said, "You went to Mr. Sullivan's office the day after the funeral, didn't you, Zanny?"

Zanny nodded. "Mr. Sullivan read me my father's will."

"While you were there, did you see any other papers that pertained to your father? Did you get a look at that file?"

Zanny shook her head. "I saw it, but that's all. It was on the desk. I saw my father's name on it, but I didn't see inside. I asked Mr. Sullivan but he wouldn't tell me. He said something about client privilege. Do you think Mr. Sullivan was murdered because of that file?"

"We're not prepared to say that," the lieutenant replied, "but the thought has certainly crossed my mind. First your father is murdered —"

Zanny frowned. "I thought you said you were treating my father's death as a suicide."

Lieutenant Jenkins nodded. "That was our first

theory. But in light of everything else we've found out about your father, we've definitely ruled out suicide. Now his lawyer has been murdered, and we found your father's file burned in the wastepaper basket in his office. Are you sure you don't know anything about that file, Zanny?"

"I'm sure."

Lieutenant Jenkins picked up his coffee cup, saw that it was empty, and set it down again. "Okay," he said. "But if you think of anything that could help me, anything at all, even if you're not sure what it means, I want you to call me. Do you still have my card?"

Zanny nodded.

As soon as Lieutenant Jenkins was gone, Zanny dressed quickly. When she went downstairs to leave the house, Mrs. Finster was making breakfast.

"Where are you going?" she asked. "Your uncle is going to be here soon."

"He won't be here for another hour," Zanny said. "I'll be back by then."

She pulled on her jacket and headed home, next door. There had to be something somewhere in the house that would give her a clue to the meaning of the slip of paper she had found in the envelope. The jumble of letters and numbers was connected to the missing ten million dollars, and she meant to do everything she could to decipher them.

She was brought up short by a man on her front lawn, hammering in a For Sale sign with a wooden mallet. A knot formed in her stomach as she watched him. With each tap of his mallet, the knot tightened, and she realized that, one way or another, she was going to have to leave this house. It would never be her home again. She walked past the real-estate man and started up the front steps.

"Hey!" the man called. "Hey, kid! Where do you think you're going? That house is empty. Nobody lives here anymore."

Zanny wrapped her fist around the key in her jacket pocket. The real-estate man's words rang in her ears. "Nobody lives here anymore. That house is empty." Empty and yet still full of her memories. She pulled the key out of her pocket and held it up so that the man could see it.

"I live here," she informed him. "This is my house. This is my father's house."

The man looked at the key. He opened his mouth to say something, then apparently thought better of it. He threw the mallet into the trunk of his car. Zanny inserted the key into the lock and then saw that the door wasn't even locked. She turned to the real-estate man, but he was already in his car. As she raised a hand to catch his attention, he pulled away from the curb. Zanny turned back to the door. Gingerly she pushed it open and then locked it again behind her. She tucked the key back into her pocket. The real-estate man must have forgotten to lock it, she told herself. Then a voice behind her said, "Good morning," and she almost jumped out of her skin. She whirled around, her heart pounding, to face Special Agent Wiley.

"What are you doing here?" she demanded.

Wiley looked around. "For a small house, this is a big house, if you know what I mean. I'm still looking. I'm going through this place with a fine-tooth comb. I'm glad you dropped by, though. It saves me a trip next door to find you."

"What for?"

"I notice you've been spending time with someone new," Wiley said.

He *noticed?* It took a moment, and then she understood. "You've been watching me?"

He shrugged apologetically. "Your father stole ten million dollars. The money was never recovered. I wouldn't be doing my job if I wasn't watching you."

Zanny shivered. A federal agent had been spying on her.

"You had dinner with a man last night. Who was he, Zanny? Do you know?"

He had been watching her last night.

"Zanny?"

"Of course I know who he is. He's my uncle."

Wiley shook his head. "I don't mean who he *says* he is. I mean who he *really* is. Do you know that?"

Zanny stared at him. What did he mean? What was he talking about?

"Do you know what your mother's maiden name was?" Wiley inquired.

"Of course I do." At least, she knew now. If he had asked her a few days ago, before her father had died, she wouldn't have known.

"It was Masters," Wiley said.

"It was Lloyd," Zanny countered.

Special Agent Wiley pulled a piece of paper from his pocket, unfolded it and handed it to her. "It was Masters. Jennifer Masters."

She stared at the piece of paper. It was a photocopy of a marriage certificate. There were two names on it: Michael Alexander and Jennifer Masters.

Slowly, Zanny shook her head. "That's not right. It wasn't Masters, it was Lloyd. Lloyd is my uncle's name. Everett Lloyd."

"Your mother's name was Masters," Wiley said. He took the paper and folded it back into his pocket. "I don't know what this Everett Lloyd character told you . . . "

"He showed me pictures. Photographs of my mother. Lots of them."

Wiley didn't look impressed. "I could show someone a photograph of you, but that wouldn't make you my sister."

What did he mean? What was he trying to tell her? "But I saw pictures of them together — of my mother and my uncle."

Wiley nodded sympathetically. "You wouldn't believe what they can do with photographs these days. You've probably seen commercials on TV, you know, the ones where actors talk to movie stars who have been dead for years. With computers, they can do anything." He dug into his pocket again and retrieved another piece of paper, which he unfolded and gave to her.

Zanny stared at it. It was a picture of her. Two pictures, actually. One of her when she was just a kid, not more than two years old. And one of her now. The second one didn't look exactly like her, but it was close enough to be eerie.

"That photo was made by a computer," Wiley

138

said. "You feed in a picture of a kid say, two years old, and the computer ages the photo and comes up with a picture of what the person would look like at fifteen or sixteen. That's how I found out your father was here, Zanny. Someone in our Intelligence Unit saw your photograph in the newspaper and matched it with that computer picture. If I could do that, don't you think someone else could, too?"

"But I saw photographs of my mother."

"You saw photographs, sure. But how do you know they were photos of your mother? You've never seen a picture of her, have you, Zanny? You have no idea what she looked like."

"She looked just like me," Zanny said. They had to be real pictures. She didn't want to believe that they weren't.

"Sometimes you see what you want to see," Wiley said softly. "That's the thing with grief. But trust me, those aren't pictures of your mother. I could show you a file. I'll have them send it to me from Washington. You can read it. You can see for yourself that your mother was a waitress from Dearborn named Jennifer Masters."

"You mean a dancer," Zanny said. "My mother was a dancer."

"She was a waitress who dreamed about being a model. Instead, she married your father."

"But my uncle said . . . "

"Jennifer Masters was an only child. Your mother didn't have any brothers or sisters."

Zanny stared at him in disbelief. "But if that's true . . . " What was going on? What was happening? "If she didn't have a brother, then . . . "

"Then this Everett Lloyd character isn't your uncle. Listen to me, Zanny. Your mother didn't have a brother. And even if she did, his name wouldn't have been Everett Lloyd."

"If he isn't my uncle," she said slowly, "who is he?"

"My guess is that he's working for Luigi Pesci."

"Luigi Pesci?" She had heard that name before.

"The head of the crime family your father stole the money from. They must have finally tracked you down."

"But that doesn't make sense. Why would my father name a criminal to be my guardian?"

"Who said he did? He named someone called Everett Lloyd as your guardian. What makes you think this guy is really Everett Lloyd?"

"The police and the Children's Aid say they've checked him out . . . "

Wiley shook his head. "The police and the Children's Aid have checked him out using information he provided. They have no reason to suspect he isn't who he says he is. But how did he turn up here? Who contacted him?"

A chill went through Zanny as she remembered what Lieutenant Jenkins had told her. "It was a coincidence," he had said. The police hadn't contacted Everett Lloyd. Everett Lloyd had contacted the police. Everett Lloyd had been looking for Zanny even before her father had died. Which meant that Wiley must be right. The Pesci family had been looking for her father.

"But it happened so long ago," she said. "You

mean that they've been looking for my father all this time? For fifteen years?"

"When ten million dollars is at stake, people have long memories. Very long memories. I bet there isn't a soldier in the family . . . "

"Soldier?"

"Foot soldier. Grunt. The guys who do the dirty work. I bet there isn't one of them who hasn't seen a picture of your father. They never stopped looking."

Zanny's stomach churned. She felt as though she was going to be sick. This was straight out of the movies. This couldn't be happening to her. It couldn't be true that her father had been hunted all this time.

"This supposed uncle of yours is looking for the same thing I am. He wants the money, and he'll do anything to get it. Anything."

Zanny stared into Wiley's grey eyes. "Do you think he . . . he's the one who . . . " She couldn't say it. She just couldn't.

"Do I think he killed your father? I think there's a better than even chance."

"Then we have to tell the police."

Wiley didn't answer right away. He looked her slowly up and down. Then slowly, almost gently, he said, "You'd like this whole thing to be over, wouldn't you, Zanny? You'd like to be able to forget about this whole mess, wouldn't you?"

Zanny nodded. She would give anything to wake up from this nightmare.

"The best way to do that," Wiley continued, "is to help me. I don't know how much your so-called uncle knows. He doesn't have the money yet, I'm sure of that. He wouldn't be hanging around here if he did. But he might have some idea where it is, or how to go about locating it. You can find that out. You can help me wrap this up once and for all."

Her father wasn't who she thought he was. Now her uncle turned out not to be her uncle.

"But the police— "

"Small-town police officers don't know how to deal with things this big, Zanny. It's not their job. But it *is* mine. If you help me find the money, I'll help the police find out who killed your father. I'll even make sure the whole story about your father stays buried, if you want me to. Nobody needs to know who Mitch Dugan really was."

Which reminded her. "I saw it in the newspaper."

"What?"

"A story about the robbery, just after it happened. I saw an article in the newspaper. At the library. But there weren't any follow-up stories."

Wiley frowned. "What do you mean?"

"When you read a newspaper article about someone stealing ten million dollars, you sort of expect there to be a follow-up story. There's weren't any. It just vanished from the news."

Wiley shrugged. "Reporters can make a real mess of things sometimes. Sometimes it's better for a case to be put under wraps to stop that from happening. So what do you say, Zanny? Will you help me out on this or not?"

"But I don't know anything."

"You lived with your father all your life. You

must have seen something. He must have said something."

Zanny thought of the note her father had left and realized that in fact he had not. Ultimately, when he'd written his final message, trying to make some kind of peace with her, he had told her absolutely nothing. She had barely known him and, he, in turn, had barely trusted her.

"Nothing," she said.

"Then keep your eyes open," Wiley said. "If you keep your eyes open, you'll learn something."

Chapter Eleven

Everett Lloyd was waiting in Mrs. Finster's living room. Zanny looked appraisingly at his rusty-coloured hair, his clear blue eyes, his placid, gentle smile. She had been so quick to trust those eyes, so eager to believe every word that came out of that gentle mouth. She had soaked up every story, every photograph. Now here he was, smiling at her again, waiting to spin another story. Well, don't hold your breath, "Uncle" Everett, she thought, because this little girl will never believe you again.

"Zanny," Mrs. Finster said reprovingly, "your uncle has been waiting for you." She set a plate of cookies in front of him and offered him more coffee. Good old Mrs. Finster. It didn't matter who showed up, or when, she always had fresh-brewed coffee and homemade cookies to offer.

"It's all right, Mrs. Finster," Everett Lloyd said. He was always so polite, so understanding. "I don't mind."

"You're here to find out what I've decided, aren't you?" Zanny asked. She tried to keep her voice calm so he wouldn't think anything was wrong, so he wouldn't know what she had found out about him. "Well, I've decided I want to stay here. You said I could stay with you, didn't you, Mrs. Finster?" Zanny looked imploringly at her neighbour. Please, don't change your mind now, she thought.

"Of course I did," Mrs. Finster replied. "I'd be happy to have you here, if you're sure that's what you want." She looked doubtfully at Everett Lloyd. Mrs. Finster likes him a lot, Zanny realized. She wants me to go with him.

"I'd like to stay here. I'm pretty sure I can find a job for the summer." She looked triumphantly at her "uncle." "There you go. Everything is settled. You don't have to worry about me. You can go back to Chicago."

Everett Lloyd smiled blandly at her over the rim of his coffee cup. "That's just what I was planning to do. Go and pack a bag, Zanny. I've booked us on a plane this afternoon. I thought this would be a good time for you to meet your new family."

"How nice," Mrs. Finster said.

"I'm not going," Zanny said.

"Zanny!" Mrs. Finster looked scandalized. "That's no way to talk to your uncle."

"I can't just pack and take off like that. I have things to do. I have friends . . . I have exams . . . " Did he think she was stupid? Did he think she would get on a plane with him and fly to Chicago, leaving behind everyone who could help her?

The benevolent smile faded from Everett Lloyd's face. "I had a long talk with Lieutenant Jenkins this morning. We both think that it would be wise to get you away from here for a while."

Mrs. Finster gasped. "You don't think she's in any danger, do you?"

"I'm afraid that's exactly what I think," Everett Lloyd said. "After everything that's happened, Zanny, I don't think we should take any chances. Pack a bag, we'll spend a few days in Chicago, and when all of this is straightened out, you can come back."

"I'll fix you a lunch for your trip," Mrs. Finster offered.

"You don't have to go to all that trouble," Everett Lloyd said. "They'll give us something on the plane."

Mrs. Finster wrinkled her nose in disgust. "Airplane food! Who can eat that? I flew to Florida last year, to visit my son the dentist. I couldn't eat the food they served me on the plane. I wouldn't feed it to a dog. I'll make you some chicken salad sandwiches. It won't take a minute."

Everett Lloyd sighed. "That's very kind of you," he said. "Go on, Zanny, get packed. We don't want to miss our flight."

Silently, Zanny climbed the stairs and dragged her suitcase out from under the bed. But instead of packing it, she pulled something from it: the note and the mysterious slip of paper her father had left. She tucked them into her jeans pocket. She went next into Mrs. Finster's room and made a quick phone call. Then she slipped down the back stairs

146

that led to the kitchen. Between the bottom of the stairs and the back door stood Mrs. Finster, buttering bread to make sandwiches. Zanny held her breath. She thought about explaining to Mrs. Finster that her uncle wasn't really her uncle, but she couldn't imagine Mrs. Finster quietly accepting that. She'd have a hundred questions, and answering them would take time that Zanny didn't have.

She heard Everett Lloyd's voice calling Mrs. Finster from the living room. Mrs. Finster heard it, too, but not as clearly.

"What?" she called. "What did you say, Mr. Lloyd?" She went into the dining room to find out. The minute her back was turned, Zanny fled.

* * *

From his vantage point at the window of the second floor bedroom next door, Special Agent Wiley saw Zanny leave Mrs. Finster's house, cut across the backyard and run down the road. He watched her progress for a few moments, then he left the house, got into his car, and followed her at a discreet distance.

* * *

Zanny drummed her fingers on the table and glanced at the clock on the wall. Where was Nick? Five minutes, he had said when she called him, but it had already been more than ten. Maybe she should have picked a meeting place farther from Mrs. Finster's house. Everett Lloyd was probably looking for her. What if he found her? What if he had somehow followed her to this restaurant and walked through the door to confront her? She would scream, she decided. There were other people in the restaurant — two middle-aged ladies drinking coffee, a silver-haired man enjoying chicken-in-a-basket, a student with a stack of library books a foot high on the table in front of him. If Everett Lloyd found her and tried to force her to leave the restaurant with him, she would scream as loudly as she could.

Bang!

Zanny jumped. Her heart hammered in her chest. What on earth . . .

The student at the table next to hers smiled sheepishly as he ducked down to retrieve a book from the floor. Zanny watched him place it on the top of the stack, then straighten all the spines so that the library labels were aligned. Slowly her heartbeat returned to normal.

Then a hand fell on her shoulder.

She opened her mouth, but the scream died in her throat. She couldn't force it out. Then she saw that she didn't have to. It wasn't Everett Lloyd looking down at her. It was Nick. He leaned over and kissed her on the cheek, then again on the mouth, leaving her breathless as he slid onto the bench opposite her.

"What's up?" he asked. "You sounded panicked on the phone. Did something happen?"

Zanny trembled as she told him about her meeting with Wiley, and about her "uncle" wanting to take her to Chicago. Nick shook his head in disbelief.

"This must be scary for you," he said. He reached for her hands and held them both in his own. "Whatever you want me to do, just ask."

She nodded gratefully. "The truth is, I'm not

really sure what I want to do. Except stay away from Everett Lloyd or whoever he really is. And find out where the money is."

"You can stay at my place," Nick offered.

"Your father won't mind?"

"He's out of town. He travels a lot. He'll be gone a couple of days, if you need a place to lie low."

Zanny smiled wanly. "I wish you could find me ten million dollars as easily as you found me a place to hide."

"If you ask me, you must be an awful lot closer to that ten million than you think you are."

"What do you mean?"

"Think about it. The Feds think you're their best chance of finding the money. And your uncle must think that you already have it or you're close to knowing where it is, or why would he want to take you back to Chicago? You know more than you think you do, Zanny."

"But I don't." Wiley had said the same thing. "I don't know anything at all. I wish I did." As she shifted on the bench, the envelope crackled in her pocket. She pulled it out and unfolded it.

"What's that?" Nick asked.

"A note. From my father." Zanny remembered exactly how she had felt as she had pulled the envelope from the book where it was hidden. She handed it to Nick.

"To be opened in the event of my death." He looked at her. "Did that lawyer give this to you?"

She shook her head. "I found it in my father's room yesterday."

Nick arched an eyebrow. "What does it say?"

"Part of it tells me that he loved me. I don't know what the other part says."

"What do you mean, you don't know?"

"Read it."

She watched him slip the two sheets of paper out of the envelope. He read her father's note to her first.

"Teddy Bear?" he said, raising his eyebrows.

Zanny blushed. "It was his pet name for me I . . . I have this birthmark . . . " Her blush deepened

Nick smiled, then unfolded the second sheet and scanned the jumble of letters and numbers. He frowned.

"It's not much help, is it?" she said when he looked up at her. "But it's everything he left me. It's all I have to go on."

"It looks like some kind of code," Nick said.

"An *unbreakable* code," Zanny said.

"You have no idea what it means?"

"None whatsoever."

"This has to be the clue we were looking for. Think, Zanny."

"I *have* been thinking. Ever since I found it, I've been trying to think what it means, but I keep coming up empty."

"You must know. You knew your father better than anyone else."

"That's not saying much. It turns out I didn't know him at all."

Nick squeezed her hand. "Hey, you're not going to get all weepy on me, are you? If we're going to crack this, you have to concentrate."

Zanny shook her head. In fact, she felt like

150

crying, but she knew it wouldn't help. All it would do was smudge her mascara.

"You know," Nick said, "when people hide things, they usually hide them someplace where they're sure they'll always have ready access. That usually means one of two things: either they hide them some place on their own property, or they hide them some place where they're sure they can always get at them."

"But we didn't find anything at my place," Zanny said.

Nick examined the letter again. He leaned back in the booth. "Then it stands to reason that he must have had another hiding place. Think, Zanny, was there any place in particular where your father liked to go? What did he do when he wasn't home?"

She didn't even have to think about it. "When he wasn't at home," she said, "he was at work." He put in such long hours that she had sometimes believed he didn't *want* to come home.

"He didn't have any hobbies?" Nick asked. "Any best buddies who he hung out with?"

"Best buddies? My father?" A couple of days ago she would have answered immediately and decisively in the negative. She would have said, "My father doesn't have any buddies at all, my father is a loner." Since the funeral, however, she realized that the way she saw him wasn't necessarily the way everyone else did. She thought about all those grateful letters from parents whose children's last days had been eased by her father. She thought about the man at the funeral who had introduced himself as her father's best friend.

"We could talk to Edward Hunter," she suggested.

"Who's he?"

"He used to work at the hospital with my father. He says he knew him well. He told me at the funeral that my father was his best friend. Maybe he'll be able to tell us something that will help us find what we're looking for."

"Good idea," Nick said. "Come on, my car's outside. Let's find him."

* * *

The librarian at the hospital had told Zanny where Edward Hunter had gone — he had bought an old house on River Street and was turning it into a hospice. She and Nick had no trouble locating the place. It wasn't at all what Zanny had expected. Scaffolding surrounded the front of the sprawling three-storey stone Victorian house, and drop cloths covered the hall floors.

"Are you sure this is the right place?" Nick asked.

"I think so." Zanny looked uncertainly up and down the main hall. The place was deserted. "The front door is open. There must be someone here."

A voice behind her said, "Can I help you?" and Zanny nearly jumped out of her skin. Clutching the sleeve of Nick's jacket, her heart hammering in her chest, she spun around to face a lanky man in tennis shoes, whom she recognized from the funeral. Edward Hunter peered at her a moment, then smiled.

"Zanny, isn't it?" he said. "Mitch's daughter."

Zanny nodded. "That's right. And this is my friend Nick Mulaney."

Edward Hunter smiled politely at Nick. "What can I do for you two?"

"Well . . ." Zanny turned to Nick for support. He nodded at her. "I was wondering if I could talk to you for a minute about my father."

The smile vanished from Edward Hunter's face. His eyes moistened. He's going to cry, Zanny realized with horror. But he didn't. He blinked a couple of times, sniffed and then forced a smile back onto his face.

"Sure," he said. "Come down to my office." He led them over drop cloths and around stepladders. "You'll have to excuse the mess around here. I know it doesn't look like it, but we're just two weeks away from opening our doors. Once it's finished, this place will be the best-equipped children's hospice in the state. And that's largely thanks to your father, Zanny. I don't know how he did it, but he was always able to get us exactly what we needed. He just went out there, found out who to talk to and then talked to them about our plans until he wore them down." Edward Hunter smiled as he opened a door and ushered them into a small office. "Your dad was a dedicated fund-raiser for this place, and the most persistent man I ever met. But I guess you knew that, didn't you?"

Zanny didn't know any of it. Her father had never mentioned this place.

"He got the workmen to agree to work six days a week so we could open as soon as possible, but even your dad couldn't get them to show up on Sunday. I guess everybody needs at least one day of rest." He circled around behind a small desk that was piled high with books — library books, Zanny guessed, by the tags on their spines — and paper. He shuffled a pile of books to one corner of the desk. "I've been studying," he explained. "There's a lot to know about running a place like this. I'm lucky I worked at the hospital library. They've let me borrow all the books I need." He smiled. "Please, have a seat."

Zanny sat in one of two chairs arranged in front of the desk. Nick claimed the other.

"So," Edward Hunter asked as he sank down into his own chair, "what do you want to know?"

What did she want to know? She hardly knew where to begin.

"You . . . you knew my father pretty well, didn't you, Mr. Hunter?"

"Call me Ed," Edward Hunter said. "Yes, I guess I knew him pretty well. I met him at a meeting."

"A meeting?"

"An AA meeting."

Zanny shook her head. She couldn't possibly have heard correctly.

"AA?" Nick said. His voice was gentle; he held Zanny's hand while he asked, "Do you mean Alcoholics Anonymous?"

Edward Hunter nodded. He looked uncomfortable. "I'm sorry, I thought you knew. I really thought . . ."

"It's okay," Nick said. He held Zanny's hand tightly. "It's okay, isn't it, Zanny?"

Zanny was too stunned to answer. Alcoholics Anonymous. Her father had been going to Alcoholics Anonymous and she had never known. All she had known was that he didn't drink. "I never touch the stuff," he would say. She wondered how it had happened: how it had started for him, and what, or who, had made him stop.

"I remember that meeting so well," Edward Hunter said, "because I had fallen off the wagon and I was making excuses for myself. The grant money I'd been counting on to get this place started had fallen through. It looked like I wasn't going to get the hospice off the ground after all. I knew that drinking wasn't going to change that, which was why I was at the meeting. I was trying to climb back onto the wagon. But it was hard, because no matter what I told myself, I knew I wasn't going to have a hospice. I wasn't going to have what I'd been working so hard for, for so long. I was just trying to make myself live with that.

"Anyway, I got talking to your father. I'd seen him around the hospital, but we hadn't really spoken. He asked me a lot of questions. He kept asking them as if the hospice was still going to happen: what are you going to do about this, how are you going to manage that, have you given any thought to this? I'd never been asked so many questions, not even on all those grant applications I'd filled out. He was so interested. When he left the meeting that night he told me, 'Keep on believing. When you believe,' he said, 'anything can happen.' I laughed at the time. I thought, sure, and maybe if I click my heels together . . . "

Zanny looked blankly at him. Edward Hunter's cheeks reddened slightly.

"You know, like Dorothy. In *The Wizard of Oz*. Anyway, three weeks later I was standing outside this building, hammering up a sign announcing the future location of the hospice. We had received an anonymous endowment from a wealthy philanthropist. Exactly two days after that, your father walked in and offered to help out."

Edward Hunter leaned back in his chair, his eyes moist again. "Your father was like a brother to me this past year, Zanny. I've worked side by side with him on this project every day for a year. I've seen him work magic with the kids at the hospital. We talked a lot. There were times, especially after, well, after one of the children passed away . . . " His eyes clouded again. "There were times when we'd talk the night away. You spend that much time with a person, you talk to them that much, and of course you think you know them. But now . . . " He shook his head. "Now that I think about it, I realize that I did most of the talking. And when he did talk, he talked about the kids or asked questions, he kept *me* talking. It was only after he died that I realized I didn't know very much about him at all. In fact, it was only recently that I found out about your brother."

Brother? The word was like a dagger in Zanny's heart. She had a brother? And no one had told her?

"It explained a lot about Mitch," Edward Hunter continued. "It explained why he was so involved in this place and why he cared so much about the kids at the hospital." His eyes clouded again. "I'm sorry," he said. "I've been rambling and I haven't really answered any of your questions. What was it you wanted to know?"

How about everything? Zanny longed to say. Because although she had known her father all her life and Edward Hunter had known him for only a year, he was way ahead of her in accumulated knowledge. He knew things about her father that she would never have guessed. He knew things that her father had never revealed to her.

"You were my father's friend," Zanny said. "I was wondering . . . did he leave anything with you?"

Edward Hunter frowned. "Leave anything? What do you mean?"

"I don't know exactly. I just thought he might have left something with you, for safekeeping."

Edward Hunter shook his head, "If you mean anything that might help to explain why . . . why he died, no. He left nothing. I can't imagine why he . . . why it happened. I'm sorry."

Zanny sighed. Seeking out this man had been a long shot, and it hadn't paid off. She started to get up.

"Are you sure?" Nick asked. "He never asked you to hold something for him?"

But Zanny wasn't listening. She was looking at the small stack of library books on Edward Hunter's desk, and at the tags taped to their spines.

QV	WQ	QZ
140.3	240	210.5
S562D	DC2	F855F
1978	F293	1989
	1993	

"An envelope maybe?" Nick said. "Or a package?"

Edward Hunter shook his head. "I'm sorry. He didn't leave anything."

Jumbles of letters and numbers. Meaningless letters and numbers that suddenly had meaning to Zanny.

"Are you sure?" Nick persisted.

"I'm sure."

"Thank you, Mr. Hunter. We have to go now," Zanny said.

Nick looked surprised. "But . . ."

"We have to go, Nick." She grabbed him by the hand and pulled him out of the office and down the hall.

"What the — " Nick began.

"You have to take me to the hospital."

His face clouded. "Why? Are you sick? What's the matter?"

"I think I know what they mean."

"What?"

"The letters and numbers. I think I know what they mean. But we have to go to the hospital."

Chapter Twelve

Zanny led Nick through the hospital's main entrance. She paused a minute to get her bearings, then said, "It's this way."

She hurried down a corridor, pushed open the door at the end of it, and started up a darkened flight of stairs to the library. Nick followed.

"Are you sure you know where you're going?" he asked. "This place looks deserted."

"It's Sunday," Zanny said. "Even a hospital is quieter than usual on Sunday."

She took the stairs two at a time. She had broken it. She had broken the code. She had deciphered the puzzle her father had left her, and now she couldn't wait to see where it would lead. At the top of the stairs, as she raced down the hall to the library, Nick at her heels, she thought about the money — ten million dollars — and wondered why, after her father had gone to all the trouble of stealing it, he hadn't spent it. It didn't make sense. She and her father had always lived in apartments or small houses. They had never taken expensive holidays; their belongings were modest. As far as Zanny knew, they had lived only on what her father managed to earn at the many low-wage jobs he had held over the years. And yet here she was, on the verge of discovering where her father had hidden a fortune.

She stopped at the library door and peered inside. The place looked empty.

"Is this it?" Nick asked. "Is this where we're going?"

She nodded.

"It's pretty quiet in there," Nick said. "Are you sure it's open?"

She tried the door. It was locked. She turned to Nick in despair.

"We have to get inside. What we're looking for is in there, I'm sure of it."

Nick pressed his face against the glass and peered inside.

"This is important, right?" he said.

She nodded.

"Very important?"

"It is to me."

Nick peeled off his leather jacket and wound it into a tight ball around his fist. "Don't try this at home, boys and girls," he said as he pulled back and hammered his fist through the glass window. Zanny stared at him in astonishment.

"Well, you said it was important."

"I'll pay to have it repaired," she said.

"If you find what you're looking for, you can pay to build them a whole new library." He reached carefully through the broken glass, unlocked the door and swung it open.

Zanny stepped inside the library and looked around. She reached into her pocket to retrieve the piece of paper with the letters and numbers on it. Nick glanced at the paper, then strode up one of the aisles of books.

"Jeez," he said, "where do we start?"

Zanny looked at the paper again. WS105.5F2P2291909.

She remembered the books on Edward Hunter's desk. The last four numbers were years, she was sure of it. 1909. She looked up at the gallery that ran around the library, and at the place where her father had liked to sit and read at lunch. She remembered what the hospital librarian had said: "We keep all the old books up there. It's sort of our archives."

"This way." She ran up the gallery steps. Nick followed.

At the top, she started checking the spines of books. QS, QV, QW, QZ, WG, WM, WQ, WS.

"Here," she said.

WS 12.

WS 52.

WS 100.

WS 102.

She was getting closer.

WS 105.

This was it.

WS 105.5.

WS 105.5F2 P229 1909.

She had found it.

She had actually found it.

She pulled a thick, hard-covered volume from the shelf.

"What is it?" Nick asked.

Zanny studied the cover. "It looks like a pediatrics textbook. Published in . . . " She flipped open the first couple of pages. " . . . 1909."

"*That's* what we're looking for? A ninety-year-old pediatrics textbook?"

She flipped through all of the pages. Nothing. She held the book by the spine and flipped the pages again. Nothing fell out.

Disappointment surged through her. She had been so sure. This had to be it. The numbers and letters matched the numbers and letters on the spine of the book. What else could the note possibly mean? There had to be something in this book that would point her in the direction of the ten million dollars. There just had to be.

"Let me see that," Nick said. He skimmed through the pages.

Nothing.

Then he held the book up to the light and examined the inside front cover. Then the inside back cover. Then the front cover again.

"What?" Zanny said. "Did you find something?"

"I'm not sure, but I think they're different."

"What's different?"

"The covers. See? The front cover is darker, it looks older. But the back-cover paper is whiter, almost as if it were newer."

"Do you think that means something?"

Nick picked at the back-cover paper with his

fingernail. He pried a corner free and peeled the paper away from its backing. Something fell to the floor with a ping.

Zanny bent to retrieve it. It was a small silver key. She held it out triumphantly to Nick.

"You did it," he said.

Zanny smiled. "*We* did it." She looked at the key again. "But what exactly did we do? What do you think it opens?"

Nick studied the key. "It looks like it belongs to a safety deposit box."

"A safety deposit box? In a bank, you mean?" Zanny slumped against the bookcase. She was so near and yet so far. She had finally found the key and she couldn't use it. All the banks were closed on Sunday.

"We can check it out tomorrow," Nick said. "Come on, let's get out of here. We can go to my place."

Zanny nodded. There was nothing else to do. She couldn't go back to Mrs. Finster's. And she had no home of her own to go to. They started down the stairs together.

"If it's a safety deposit box key, it must be for a bank in town, don't you think?" she said. "We could . . ."

The words died in her throat. There was a man standing just inside the library entrance.

"What's he doing here?" Nick asked. "How did he find us?"

Zanny shook her head. Her mouth went dry. Beside her, Nick tensed. Everett Lloyd's face was grim beneath his red hair as he strode toward them.

"Hold it," Nick said. Ordered. "That's far enough, pal. Don't come any closer." His voice had become sharp, authoritative. Zanny glanced at him. She had never seen such determination in his eyes.

Everett Lloyd halted a couple of metres away. He studied Nick a moment, then turned his pale blue eyes on Zanny.

"Are you letting your friend tell you what to do now, Zanny?"

Zanny didn't answer.

Everett Lloyd shrugged. "Okay, if that's the way you want it. But let me ask you something."

"I don't have to talk to you," Zanny said. "And I don't have to listen to you."

"How long have you known your friend Nick? I bet you haven't known him very long."

"You heard what she said," Nick growled. "She's not interested in listening to you."

"In fact," Everett Lloyd continued smoothly, looking only at Zanny, his eyes boring into her, "I bet you two just got to know each other recently. You met Nick just before your father died, isn't that right, Zanny?"

"Listen, pal —" Nick began.

"Nick is my friend," Zanny said. "He's been helping me."

"Helping you what? Helping you find the ten million dollars?"

Zanny said nothing.

"Think about it, Zanny," Everett Lloyd continued. "Your picture appeared in the newspaper a week before your father was killed. That picture is the reason I'm here."

"So you said," she replied.

"You don't have to talk to this creep, Zanny," Nick said. "Let's get out of here."

"If I saw that picture, a lot of other people could have seen it, too," Everett Lloyd said. "Come on, Zanny, I'm right, aren't I? Nick is a recent friend, isn't he? You just met him, didn't you?"

"Come on, Zanny," Nick said.

"I bet you never even saw Nick until about two weeks ago, am I right?"

Eleven days, Zanny thought. Exactly eleven days ago, Nick Mulaney walked into her algebra class. But that didn't mean anything. There was no reason for her to listen to anything Everett Lloyd said.

"What do you know about him, Zanny?" Everett Lloyd inquired. "Have you met his parents? I bet you haven't. And do you know why? Because he hasn't lived with them since he was sixteen. That was how many years ago now, Nick? Seven years, isn't it?"

Zanny stared at Nick. Seven years ago? But that would make him . . . twenty-three.

"Go ahead, Nick," Everett Lloyd said. "Prove me wrong. Show her your driver's licence. Let her see for herself how old you are."

Zanny searched Nick's chocolate eyes, but found nothing in them to reassure her.

"It would be really interesting to take a look at that driver's licence, Zanny," Everett Lloyd said. "Because you'd see the name on it as well as the birth date. You'd find out that your good friend here isn't Nick Mulaney at all. That *is* the name you gave the school, isn't it — Nick Mulaney? Well, his name isn't Mulaney. It's Pesci. His grandfather is Luigi Pesci, the man your father took the ten million from in the first place." Everett Lloyd held a hand out. "Come with me, Zanny. Come with me now."

Nick's hand closed on her upper arm.

"I don't know what you're trying to pull, pal, but she's not going anywhere with you. She doesn't believe a word you've said, isn't that right, Zanny?"

Zanny stared at the red-haired man with his hand extended to her. She had no reason to believe him. He had lied to her. He had lied to the police. He wasn't who he said he was. And now he was just trying to confuse her by claiming Nick wasn't who *he* said he was. Well, she would show him. She turned to Nick.

"Let me see your driver's license," she said. She looked evenly at Everett Lloyd. Maybe he thought he could scare her with his lies, but he couldn't. She would show him.

"Zanny, for pete's sake . . . " Nick protested.

"Go ahead, let her see it, Nick," Everett Lloyd said.

"Stay out of this!" Nick shouted. His voice was so loud it made Zanny jump. His hand clamped around her arm. "We're leaving. Come on."

"Nick, you're hurting me."

But he didn't let go.

"What's the matter, Nick?" Everett Lloyd taunted. "Aren't you going to show us your driver's licence?"

"I told you to stay out of this!" Nick roared.

"Nick . . ." Confused, Zanny started to pull away from him. But he held on. His fingers bit into her arm.

"Nick, let me go."

"Yeah, Nick," Everett Lloyd said, "let her go."

Zanny gasped. He had produced a gun from somewhere, and was pointing it directly at Nick. Before she could do more than absorb this fact, Nick yanked her in front of him, one arm clamped around her like a vice. Suddenly, Zanny felt something press against her left temple. Something cold and hard.

"Drop the gun," Nick ordered, his voice a low growl in her ear, "or you can kiss her goodbye."

The chill started in Zanny's chest and radiated out in waves until she was frozen all over. This couldn't be happening.

"Nick, please . . ." She tried to pull free of him, but his arm was like a steel band around her. This was no joke. This was for real. The floor tipped and whirled beneath her. She felt as if she was going to be sick. This couldn't be happening. They were lying to her — they had all been lying to her — her father, Everett Lloyd and now Nick. All any of them cared about was the money.

Everett Lloyd still held his gun, but now he aimed it at Zanny. His face was grim.

Nick repeated his demand, forming each word carefully. "Put the gun down."

Everett Lloyd loosened his grip on the gun. He stooped slowly. Zanny tensed. What if he tried something? And what if Nick lived up to his word? Everett Lloyd set the gun down onto the floor. Metal

167

clicked against tile. Then he straightened.

Zanny felt the mouth of the gun move away from her right temple. Nick wasn't aiming at her any more, he was drawing a bead on Everett Lloyd. Everett Lloyd realized it, too. He had already straightened up when he saw the gun swinging toward him.

Everett Lloyd looked at the gun, then at Nick. "You're going to kill me? Here? In a hospital?" He glanced around the library. "And then what? You kill her, too?" He looked at Zanny. "If he kills me, he'll have to kill you, too, Zanny. Think about it. You'll be a witness. You'll be the only person who saw him shoot an unarmed man."

Nick's gun came up a little higher.

"No!" Zanny shouted.

She stomped down with one heel on Nick's foot. She aimed for the instep, where she would do the most harm. At the same time, she threw her whole weight against his grip.

Nick cursed loudly and released her. She slammed into the wall. Then she heard a sound, a whispering sound followed by a dull thud. She looked at Everett Lloyd who was staring empty-handed at Nick, his gun still on the floor at his feet. Then she looked at Nick. Blood had blossomed on the front of his T-shirt. His face held a look of complete surprise. He hung a moment in the air, as if a huge hand had him by the back of the collar and was holding him there. Then, suddenly, as if released, he collapsed.

My God, Zanny thought. My God.

Everett Lloyd stooped to retrieve his gun. Then

a voice from the far end of the room said, "Don't do it, Lloyd."

Special Agent Wiley, his gun drawn, was standing just inside a door marked Exit. Zanny had never been so happy to see anyone in her life.

"Very carefully, Lloyd, I want you to kick that gun away from you," Wiley said. "*Very* carefully."

Slowly, with a reluctance Zanny could read on his face, Everett Lloyd complied. The gun skidded across the floor.

"Good," Wiley said. He kept his eyes and his weapon steady on Everett Lloyd as he said, "Now, Zanny, I want you to pick up that gun and bring it to me."

Zanny's legs trembled as she struggled to her feet. Nick lay in front of her, motionless, dead or dying. Part of her wanted to go to him, to touch him, to touch his soft lips. Anguish wrenched her heart. She had trusted him. She had depended on him. She didn't want to believe that he'd lied to her, had been lying to her since the day he had ambushed her outside the school.

"Zanny?" Special Agent Wiley said. "Do you hear me?"

Mutely, Zanny nodded. Her knees shook so hard that she had to hold a hand against the wall to steady herself.

"Get the gun, Zanny," Wiley instructed. He spoke slowly, as if speaking to a small child.

Zanny moved toward the weapon on uncertain legs. She couldn't look at Nick; she refused to look at Everett Lloyd.

"Pick it up by the barrel," Wiley continued.

"That's it, slow and easy. Bring it to me."

She started toward him.

"Don't do it, Zanny," Everett Lloyd called from behind her. "Don't give him the gun. You can't trust him any more than you could trust Nick."

Zanny turned slowly and stared at him. Rage boiled in her as she looked at the red-haired man. "Are you going to tell me he isn't who he says he is either?" she demanded. "That he isn't a DEA agent? Because if you are, you can forget it. I'm not listening to you. Why should I? *You* aren't who you say you are. You aren't my uncle."

"That's right, Zanny," Wiley coaxed. "Don't listen to him, just bring the gun here."

"I don't know what he's been telling you, Zanny," Everett Lloyd said, "but I am your uncle. And I was your father's partner."

"His partner?"

"When he was a cop. That's how he met your mother. I introduced them."

"You're lying, Lloyd," Wiley said. "I've told her all about you."

"I don't know what he told you, Zanny. But if he told you your father was a thief, he lied to you. That's not the way it happened."

"Why don't you shut up?" Wiley snarled. "Shut up before I— "

"Before you what, Wiley? Before you shoot an unarmed man in front of a witness? Or are you planning to kill her, too, and claim self-defence?"

Wiley's slate-grey eyes were as cold as stone.

"Just after you were born, your father left the police force and joined the DEA. He went undercover for them," Everett Lloyd said. "Wiley was his contact. Wiley was the one who was supposed to back him up, to look after him, to make sure his cover wasn't blown."

"Shut up," Wiley ordered. "Shut up."

"But somehow something went wrong, isn't that right, Wiley? Something went wrong and the next thing anyone knew, your father's car was blown up. Except that your father wasn't in it, your mother was. That's how your mother died, Zanny. She was blown up by a car bomb. That's when your father decided to get even. He decided to hit the Pesci family, Luigi Pesci in particular, in the only place it would really hurt them — in the wallet, and in their pride. Wiley was supposed to back him up on that one, too, weren't you, Wiley?"

"I'm warning you, Lloyd, if you don't shut up . . ."

"Your father moved in on a major drug buy. He waited until the Pescis had traded ten million dollars worth of drugs for cash. Then he held up the Pescis. He humiliated them by stealing the money right out from under their noses. Wiley was in on that operation, weren't you, Wiley? If I'm not mistaken, you co-ordinated the whole thing, didn't you?"

Wiley came a step closer.

"And then something went wrong. Something unexpected happened, isn't that right, Wiley? What was it? Did Mike realize what you planned to do? He guessed you were going to run with the money yourself, didn't he? And he stopped you dead in your tracks. Stopped you dead and then had to take off with the kid to protect himself from Pesci, from the DEA and most of all from you, isn't that right, Wiley?"

Wiley stretched out his hand to Zanny. "Bring me the gun," he said.

Zanny hesitated. If Everett Lloyd really was her uncle, then Wiley had lied to her. Or Everett Lloyd was lying to her now, and Wiley was telling the truth.

Everett Lloyd's pale eyes caught and held Zanny's. "I know things about you that no one else knows. I know that when you were a baby, you never liked to go to sleep. I can't tell you how many nights I walked the floor with you, when your mother used to rope me into babysitting."

"Don't listen to him, Zanny. Give me the gun," Wiley urged her.

"I know you have a birthmark," Everett Lloyd said. "On your right . . . on your behind. Shaped like a little bear. That's why when you were little, your father used to call you Teddy."

Zanny almost lost her grip on the gun barrel. She peered into his eyes: they were the same colour as the eyes that had stared out from the photos he had shown her of the girl who was her mother. "They can fake photographs in ways you'd never be able to detect with the naked eye," Wiley had told her. "They can do incredible things with computers these days," he had said. But what could they do with birthmarks? What computer in the world could spit out her father's pet name for her?

Zanny had been less than two years old when her father had dropped out of sight. What kind of information could anyone have gathered about her before that? Why would anyone have bothered? Was this really the kind of world where the good guys or the bad guys or any guys at all, for that matter, kept files on babies, on their birthmarks, on their pet names, just in case? She tightened her hand around the barrel of the gun; in her other hand, she held the key she had found inside the library book.

Wiley raised his gun to draw a more accurate bead on Everett Lloyd. His grey eyes squinted down to pinpoints.

"I found it," Zanny said. She held the key out in front of her so that both men could see it. "I found the money. It's in a safety deposit box. Here's the key."

Wiley moved a step closer. He kept his gaze focused on Everett Lloyd, but glanced hungrily every so often at the key.

"Give it to me, kid. Give me the key."

Zanny smiled. "Sure," she replied. "Here." She threw the key in Wiley's direction, aiming long and high, over his head. He had to turn to follow its arc. And in that split second, as he followed his greed, she tossed the gun to Everett Lloyd. Then everything kicked into slow motion, as if she had stumbled into a movie dream sequence. A deadly dream sequence.

Wiley's head swung back to follow the arc of the key, not for long, but long enough for Everett Lloyd to get a grip on the gun.

"Down!" he shouted at Zanny. "Get down!"

In the instant that Zanny scrambled out of the way and flung herself down, the key clicked to the tile. It skidded along the waxed floor. Wiley started to swing back to Everett Lloyd, his gun coming up with every degree he turned. Everett Lloyd stepped back and to the side, toward the wall. Zanny couldn't believe it. She was in the middle of a shootout. Two men were facing each other right in front of her — two men aiming deadly weapons at each other.

Two shots rang out. They came close together, but Zanny was pretty sure that Wiley had got his off first. Everett Lloyd slammed back against the wall with the impact. His gun clattered to the floor. Special Agent Wiley raised his gun again. Zanny felt ice run through her. She saw Everett Lloyd, his face white with shock and pain, stagger toward his fallen weapon. Zanny dove across the hallway then, to where Nick was lying, and tore the gun from Nick's still hand. Then, like a rock hitting the surface of a pond, Wiley dropped. He fell forward on the tile; she heard the crack of his forehead on the hard surface. The back of his jacket was drenched with blood. A second later, Everett Lloyd fell too.

Chapter Thirteen

Zanny poured cream into her coffee and watched it billow like clouds in a stormy sky. She hadn't slept all night. There had been so much to think about. So much had shifted and then shifted again, in such a short period of time. The whole geography of her life had changed. She needed a map to reorient herself. But at least she was confident that she now had one she could trust.

Across the table from her, Everett Lloyd — Uncle Everett —was trying to cut a piece of ham with the side of his fork. He wasn't having much luck.

"Here," Zanny said. She took his fork from him, and his knife, and cut the ham into bite-sized pieces.

His face was pale; his left arm hung, useless, in a sling. But he must have been feeling better because he attacked his ham and eggs with enthusiasm. Zanny wondered what his wife — her Aunt Margaret — was like, and what it would be like living with two small cousins. "You're going to have to brace yourself," her uncle had told her at the hospital. "Our side of the family may be small, but Margaret's is huge. We have to rent extra chairs to seat everyone at Thanksgiving. And Christmas — what a party!" Zanny couldn't imagine it. Her holidays had all been so quiet, so small — Christmas for two.

Her uncle glanced at her as he drank his coffee. "Nervous?" he asked.

"I just wish he'd get here," Zanny said. Lieutenant Jenkins had arranged to meet them in here, across the street from the bank where her father had rented a safety deposit box.

"Don't worry," he said. "I have a feeling that Lieutenant Jenkins is a pretty punctual guy." He smiled gently at her.

"But what if we find it? What if we really find the ten million dollars?"

Her uncle shrugged. "Then we can close the book on this thing once and for all. Your father was a good man, Zanny. He had some tough times in his life, really tough, first after your brother died, then after your mother was killed. But he was a good man and I think he meant well. We can concentrate on that for a while, and forget the rest of it."

Zanny gazed down at her coffee for a moment, then up again into her uncle's pale eyes. "I didn't know until yesterday that I had a brother."

Everett Lloyd reached across the table and squeezed her hand. "I'm sorry. There's just so much to catch up on, so many blanks to fill in for you. We haven't had much time together yet."

Zanny nodded and fought back tears of frustration. "What happened to him?"

"He had leukemia. He died when he was five years old. It was a long death, Zanny, and a hard one, for both your mother and your father, but especially for your father. He had a lot of problems after Alex died."

Alex. She had had a brother once, named Alex.

"Mike started to drink. He started volunteering for the most dangerous assignments. I was a cop then, too, and I knew what it was like working undercover. And your dad, well, it was like he needed to be right out there, right on the edge. I think that's why he joined the DEA. I think that's why he volunteered for the Pesci assignment. And after your mother was killed . . . " His voice trailed off. He sighed. "But even with everything that happened, he came through. He did the right thing, Zanny. He protected you. He quit drinking. He held down a good job where people respected him. And that's what people are going to remember about your father, Zanny. They're going to remember the good things."

"Who killed him?" Zanny asked. "Wiley, or Nick?"

"Wiley. I don't think he meant to. He must have seen your picture in the paper and traced you here. I think he was trying to find out where the money was, and your father surprised him. They must have struggled, and your father was killed accidentally. Wiley would have been foolish to kill him without first finding out what he had done with the money."

"And Wiley killed Mr. Sullivan, too?"

Everett Lloyd nodded. "Apparently. But according to what police forensics have turned up, Sullivan was the one who burned your father's file. And from what remained of it in the waste paper basket, he had burned it well *before* he died, before Wiley got to him."

"But why? Why would Mr. Sullivan burn my father's file?"

Everett Lloyd shrugged. He washed down the last of his ham and eggs with a mouthful of black coffee. "You've got me there," he said. "Probably because there was something in it he didn't want anyone to see. You know, Zanny, it's possible that there are some things we'll never know."

Loose ends. There were too many loose ends. Too many questions raised, only to be left unanswered. Zanny took a sip of her own coffee.

"Why did Wiley tell me you weren't my uncle?"

"To keep you off balance. To make sure that if you did find the money, he would be the only person you'd tell. He wanted it for himself, Zanny. That was what he wanted fifteen years ago, and it's what he wanted yesterday." Her uncle glanced at the door. "There's the lieutenant." He consulted his watch, which he now wore awkwardly on his right wrist. "Right on time, just like I thought."

Zanny frowned and saw Lieutenant Jenkins coming toward them. Her heart began to hammer in her chest. In a few minutes, she would be unlocking her father's safety deposit box. Unlocking the past.

* * *

It took longer than she expected. There was more paperwork involved than Zanny ever thought possible: first the court and legal papers that Lieutenant Jenkins produced, and then the sheaf of forms, which first Lieutenant Jenkins and then Zanny had to sign, three copies of each. When the box was finally brought to them in a small cubicle, Zanny was surprised to see how small it was, how flat, how light and easy to carry. She couldn't imagine what it could contain that would be worth ten million dollars. Her spirits sagged. Another loose end. Another question that would be left unanswered.

Lieutenant Jenkins produced the safety deposit box key from his pocket. He started to insert it into the lock, then stopped and offered it to Zanny. Her hands shook as she took the key and slowly unlocked the box. She stared at the box for a moment, then closed her eyes and whispered a prayer as she flipped the top up. When she looked again, all she saw was an envelope and a small book bound in red leather, with a note attached to it by an elastic band. She looked at Lieutenant Jenkins and at her uncle, who nodded. She reached first for the envelope. On it someone, her father, she supposed, had typed *To Everett Lloyd, or to the Authorities, in the event of my death.* Zanny held it a moment; it was thick with paper. She handed it to her uncle.

He read the words on the front, then hooked a finger under one of the flaps and ripped the envelope open. He pulled out a sheaf of typewritten papers. As he began to read them, Zanny reached for the leather-bound book. She slipped the elastic band from it and unfolded the note. It was brief and written in her father's hand.

179

*Zanny: Your mother wanted you to have
this. It isn't much, but it's yours. She loved
you very much. Dad.*

Zanny opened the book. It was a diary. She
didn't recognize the hand it was written in. It wasn't
her father's loopy sprawl. This was neat, close,
elegant script in navy ink. "To my darling baby
daughter," it began. The first page was inscribed
with a date that had always been important to Zanny:
her birthday. Her eyes brimmed with tears. After a
lifetime of wondering what it would sound like,
Zanny was finally hearing her mother's voice.
Reading her mother's thoughts. She flipped through
the book and found, finally, the place where it
ended. She read the date of the last entry: two
months before Zanny's second birthday.

Beside her, her uncle sighed. He handed the
sheaf of papers he had been reading to Lieutenant
Jenkins.

"Well, I guess that answers two questions,"
Everett Lloyd said. "Why Mr. Sullivan burned the
file, and what happened to the ten million dollars
your father took from the Pesci family."

Zanny closed the diary and held it close to her
heart. She looked at her uncle.

"It seems that your father used the money to
endow a hospice for children," he informed her.

"Edward Hunter's hospice," Zanny said. It
made perfect sense. Just after Edward Hunter met
her father, an anonymous donor had provided all the
money he needed to start his hospice for terminally
ill children. Her father spent his spare time at the
hospital visiting and cheering up children who were

desperately ill. Her own little brother had died of leukemia. It all fit. That was where the ten million dollars had gone. That was what he had spent it on. That was why, after so many years, he had started to relax in Birks Falls. What a shame it was that he had found peace too late.

Lieutenant Jenkins nodded. "Your father writes here that he didn't think about what he would do with the money before he took it. All he thought about was revenge. He says it was only when he came here and met Edward Hunter that he finally knew what the money was for."

"He had William Sullivan draw up the papers," her uncle said. "One of the terms was that the name of the donor remain anonymous."

"Which was why Mr. Sullivan burned the file," Zanny said. "So that the information would stay secret."

Her uncle nodded.

"But why was Mr. Sullivan killed?" Zanny persisted.

"He was protecting your father's secret," Jenkins said. "That's why he burned the file. Wiley killed him trying to get that secret out of him."

Lieutenant Jenkins folded the papers back into the envelope. "I don't know what the Feds are going to say about this, but if you ask me, he couldn't have found a better place to use the money. The hospice will mean a lot to a lot of families."

A tear slipped down Zanny's cheek. She thought she had known her father: she had known so little.

* * *

Everett Lloyd glanced out the window. "That's our taxi," he said.

"Wait!" called Mrs. Finster. She scurried out of the kitchen and pressed an enormous brown paper bag into Zanny's hands. "I made you a snack. It's a long plane ride. You'll be hungry."

"But they'll feed us on the plane, Mrs. Finster," Zanny protested.

Mrs. Finster wrinkled her nose in disdain. "I made you some of my chicken salad sandwiches. And some cookies. And, Mr. Lloyd, I remembered how much you liked those cookies, so I wrote down the recipe for your wife. It's in with the cookies."

"Thank you, Mrs. Finster," Zanny's uncle said. "Thank you for everything."

Mrs. Finster looked at Zanny, then suddenly threw herself at her, capturing her in a bear hug.

"Good luck, dear," she said. Her eyes watered. She wiped them with the corner of her apron. "Look at me," she said with a laugh. "My boys always say I cry at the drop of a hat. I guess they're right."

Zanny smiled. "I appreciate everything you've done for me, Mrs. Finster. I really do."

"It was nothing. Anyone would have done the same."

"Maybe," Zanny replied. "But you're the one who did, and I want you to know how much I appreciate it." She leaned forward and kissed Mrs. Finster on the cheek.

Mrs. Finster blushed. "Well, I guess you two had better get going." Then she perked up. "Oh! It's such a long flight. Let me get you some magazines to read on the plane."

"It's okay," Zanny said. She felt the reassuring bulk of the leather-bound diary in her purse. She had read every word of it last night. She intended to read it again. She intended to keep on reading it until she had every word committed to memory. "I already have something to read."

"Something good, I hope," Mrs. Finster said.

"Something *very* good," Zanny assured her.